She was in trouble.

The firm set of Nicco's mouth told her he was angry with her.

Scout went on the offensive. "Say something. Anything."

"You handled yourself today. But what's going to happen when you find yourself in a situation you can't handle?"

A dozen retorts came to mind. She rejected all but one. "I can't stop living my life because of some threats."

"You could have been killed."

And then she understood. He'd been afraid. For her.

"I'm sorry for scaring you."

"Nothing is worth your life. Nothing. Including this investigation."

Scout wanted to protest, but she didn't want to destroy the fragile peace that hovered between them. "I'll be more careful. I promise."

"I don't want you to just be careful. I want you to stay alive. Because next time..."

Nicco let the words trail off. He didn't need to speak them. The silent warning echoed in her head.

Next time the job wouldn't go unfinished. It'd end with her death.

Jane M. Choate dreamed of writing from the time she was a small child when she entertained friends with outlandish stories complete with happily-ever-after endings. Writing for Love Inspired Suspense is a dream come true. Jane is the proud mother of five children, grandmother to seven grandchildren and the staff to one cat who believes she is of royal descent.

Books by Jane M. Choate

Love Inspired Suspense

HIGH-RISK INVESTIGATION

JANE M. CHOATE

HARLEQUIN® LOVE INSPIRED® SUSPENSE

Recycling programs
for this product may
not exist in your area.

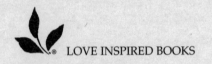 LOVE INSPIRED BOOKS

ISBN-13: 978-1-335-54360-8

High-Risk Investigation

Copyright © 2018 by Jane M. Choate

www.Harlequin.com

Printed in U.S.A.

Fear thou not; for I am with thee: be not dismayed;
for I am thy God: I will strengthen thee; yea,
I will help thee; yea, I will uphold thee with the right hand
of my righteousness.
—*Isaiah* 41:10

To my mother, Georgia Sampson McBride,
and to my sister, Carla Sue Berger, each of whom
waged a valiant fight against ovarian cancer, and to all the
women and those who love them who battle this disease.

ONE

Nicco Santonni yanked at the too-tight collar of the starched white shirt. The tuxedo, a rental, felt like a straitjacket that at any moment might strangle him. He'd take a flak jacket or even the *shalwar kameez*—the traditional Middle Eastern baggy, pajama-like trousers paired with a long cotton tunic—over the monkey suit, but tonight's job dictated formal wear.

He had as much use for a tuxedo as he did for the glitz and glamour of the ballroom at Savannah's premiere hotel, but a bodyguard went where his client did and tonight that meant showing up for a charity fund-raiser.

He'd arrived early for the event. Another operative was watching the client in the hours before the gala began. Ranger to the core, he'd wanted to survey his surroundings. He didn't like being taken by surprise. Constructing a grid pattern of the ballroom came first, followed by identifying any likely spots for a sniper attack. He didn't expect to use his expertise in explosives or hand-to-hand combat tonight, but an operative for S&J Security/Protection never knew what he or she would be called upon to do.

Protecting a client required finesse and a boatload of other skills, but protecting one who didn't know she was being guarded presented the distinct problem of keeping close without giving himself away. Not for the first time, Nicco wondered how he'd ended up with a job he didn't want.

The answer was simple. Family. His brother Sal's wife, Olivia, had asked that he protect Scout McAdams.

Olivia had stressed that her friend not know she was under S&J's protection until it became absolutely necessary. "I know Scout. She'll tell you to get lost. But the letters she's been receiving are getting scarier all the time. I'm worried."

Nicco couldn't say no. Not to Olivia. She was family, and family was everything to the Santonnis. Family, and loyalty to the people who signed your paycheck.

Working for S&J had been the best thing to happen to him after he'd left the Rangers. Named for the founders, Shelley Rabb Judd and her brother Jake Rabb, S&J was quickly becoming a leading player in the growing protection industry with clients in both the private and public sectors.

Nicco had never regretted the decision to join the firm. Caring was the cornerstone of S&J. That, and passion for the job. He liked the work and sometimes even liked the clients. As Shelley said, "You don't have to like the clients. You just have to protect them."

He didn't know whether he liked Scout McAdams as he'd never been introduced to her. He knew she was a reporter and that she had been receiving threats. His lips tightened. Whoever was threatening McAdams was just a bully, and if there was one thing Nicco was good at, it was protecting innocents from bullies. He'd encountered his share in Afghanistan—warlords who ordered death as easily as an ordinary person would order coffee.

As unobtrusively as possible, Nicco conducted a scan of the area surrounding his client. Accustomed to searing heat, blowing sand and the smells of war, he found the scents of perfume and flowers cloying. He watched as McAdams worked her way through the crowd, moving quickly with a self-assurance that belied her pint-size frame, her gold dress swirling about her ankles. There was an intensity to her that attracted attention, while the determination in her stride had people stepping aside to make way for her.

A pendant in the shape of a miniature gold pencil swayed gently as she walked. He'd noticed earlier that she occasionally touched it as one might a talisman and wondered at the significance of it.

The hair at the back of his neck prickled, and an unmistakable rush of adrenaline propelled his senses to high alert. A fraction of a moment later, he settled into a state of cool calm. His breathing slowed, steadied, as he assessed the possible risks.

Protecting the client came first. Always. He did not make a move for the Walther that he wore in a custom-fit shoulder holster. It was enough to know that it was within reach should he need it. A backup piece fit snugly at his ankle.

The weapons were a far cry from the M249 SAW, a light machine gun, and the 9 mm Berretta he'd carried as an Army Ranger, but they did the job. A half smile tipped the corners of his lips as he pictured the probable reaction of tonight's well-heeled crowd if he'd appeared with the submachine gun cradled in his arms.

Whether in the mountains of Afghanistan or the ballroom of a glitzy hotel, preparation was key. For Nicco, that meant being ready to do whatever it took to get the job done, including using deadly force if necessary.

Violence didn't solve problems. Too often, it created them. But to assume that the world's wrongs could be fixed with a bunch of talk was not only naive, it was dangerous.

He moved closer to McAdams, observing the ebb and flow of people closest to his client as well as any place where a sniper might take position. A glint of metal from the balcony caught his eye. He didn't need to see the gun to know that a shooter was taking aim.

Nicco was in the cold zone now, the state that allowed him to be part of the moment without being in the moment. Instinct and training took over.

"Everybody down." He didn't wait to see if people obeyed but sprang toward his client just as two shots fired in rapid succession. He knocked her down and covered her body with his own.

Screams and cries echoed throughout the cavernous room. Nicco ignored those, his concern for only the woman he'd flattened. He hoped he hadn't injured her, but he'd had to get her out of the range of fire as quickly as possible.

Cautiously, he rolled off her, then motioned for her to crawl beneath one of the high-top tables set up in the ballroom. Though his instincts told him to go after the shooter, his first duty lay with the client.

When no other shots sounded, he climbed out from under the table, looked about, then offered his hand to Scout McAdams. "Are you all right?"

"Yes," she said, placing her hand in his. "I think you just saved my life."

* * *

"Rachel Scout McAdams," she said, sticking out her hand.

"Nicco Santonni."

"Thank you, Mr. Santonni. I owe you."

"You don't owe me a thing."

The brusqueness of the response startled her. Maybe, she reasoned, he was as shaken by the shots as she had been. She snuck a glance at him and dismissed that thought. The big man standing in front of her didn't appear to be the kind to be rattled by anything or anyone.

Scout took inventory of her injuries. Throbbing hip and shoulder. Sore chest, probably bruised ribs. No doubt about it—she was going to hurt tomorrow. For now, the rush of adrenaline kept the worst of the pain at bay. Resigning herself to the nightmares the sound of gunshots would trigger, she did her best to ignore the prospect of a sleepless night.

Breathe.

She shoved aside images from the past and focused on the here and now. Delayed panic swept through the ballroom, sobs and cries punctuating the overall confusion. Sirens screeched in the distance, but the immediate danger appeared to be over. At least she hoped so.

Brushing herself off, she eyed the man who had pushed her down and covered her body with his own when the shots had pierced the buzz of party chatter. She'd hugged the floor, concentrating on breathing, not an easy task when a two-hundred-pound man had just flattened her with the force of a battering ram.

Not that she was complaining. He'd saved her life.

Only when the big man had rolled off her had she been able to move and seek protection beneath a table as he'd ordered. Her pulse had still been in overdrive, her legs shaking when she'd gotten to her feet. Annoyance at herself poured through her. She wasn't some weak-kneed wimp who fainted at the first hint of violence. She stiffened her shoulders and took stock of her surroundings.

The rancid smells of fear and panic overrode the perfumed air of the ballroom as people scrambled for exits.

Breathe.

"It's all right," she murmured to a bleating woman who had collapsed in a nearby chair. "Nobody was hurt." She prayed that was true. She stayed by the lady's side until her husband found her and took her in his arms.

Scout turned and felt her rescuer's gaze on her, considering.

"You've had a shock, but you took the time to help someone else."

After the coldness of his tone, the warmth in the words surprised her. "She was frightened. I didn't want her to be alone." Scout had more reason than most to know what that felt like.

"What about you? You had to be scared."

"I was plenty scared." Goose bumps puckered her arms in confirmation.

She studied the man, not bothering trying to hide her interest. He looked as out of place at this yawn-fest as she felt. As a reporter, she was accustomed to expecting the unexpected. Being thrown to the ground by a man who looked as though he could have stepped right out of a romance novel definitely qualified as unexpected.

Tall, rangy, with dark good looks that hinted at Italian ancestry, he had some impressive moves. Ex-military, she guessed. Maybe special ops. He resembled the cops and soldiers she'd come across while hunting down stories: clean-cut, physically fit, with experience sharpening his gaze.

Nearly black eyes, a sharp blade of a nose and lips on the full side made for an arresting face, one too unique for mere handsomeness. The dark tux, pristine white shirt and precisely knotted tie should have detracted from the air of controlled power that he wore so easily, but the elegance had the opposite effect. He looked dangerous.

Get it together, girl. She had no business cataloging the man's features, no matter how attractive he might be.

She'd been making her way to Leonard Crane, the man she'd been trying to interview for the last couple of weeks, when the shots had ripped through the air. Crane was the boss of Savannah's sanitation/waste union.

Scout knew she was running a risk in continuing where her mother, a true-crime writer with eleven bestsellers to her credit, had left off in investigating murders in the labor unions. Though she couldn't prove it, she believed her mother had been killed because of her research. Scout and her father had been collateral damage. Scout had recovered from the bullet to her shoulder, but her father had died. The police had called it a carjacking gone wrong.

Scout knew differently.

According to her mother's notes, Crane had known the four bosses who had been murdered in the last two years. Her mother had believed that he was connected to the murders, either directly or indirectly. Scout wasn't about to let go of the best lead she had.

Finding out that Crane was going to be present at the Homes for Everyone fund-raiser had been a bonus. It made up—almost—for shelling out a week's pay for a dress she'd probably never wear again. Being assigned to cover the affair still rankled.

Her nose wrinkled. Give her a juicy case of corruption to investigate and she was there. She'd paid her dues in covering rubber-chicken dinners and was now slowly working her way up from the society page to the city page, from fluff to hard news. It felt like a demotion to be assigned to something like this.

The police arrived. She figured they'd surround the hotel, block exits, and forbid anyone from entering or leaving. It was too bad the gunman had probably already made his escape, rendering such procedures useless.

Scout answered the questions a detective fired at her as briefly as she could and kept her thoughts to herself. Maybe she was jumping to conclusions. Just because she'd gotten a few pieces of hate mail threatening her life if she didn't back off her investigation, didn't mean she was a target.

Scout McAdams was rarely dishonest with herself, but right now, she recognized that she was indulging in a moment of being just that.

"You're certain you have nothing else to add, Ms. McAdams?" the detective asked for the fifth time.

Nicco Santonni hovered nearby. His presence

was a comfort, and though she didn't want to admit it, she welcomed it.

"I'm certain." Irritation at the repetitive questions and a large dose of residual fear sharpened her voice.

"If you think of anything…"

"I know where to find you."

The detective nodded curtly and turned his attention elsewhere.

Red-gold hair swung past her shoulders, framing a heart-shaped face with intelligent eyes and a full mouth. Her girl-next-door looks were far more appealing than the elaborate hair and makeup favored by many of the women present. But it wasn't her beauty that demanded and held attention; it was the determination that sparked in her eyes.

Scout McAdams had a reputation for doing whatever it took to get a story.

Deliberately, Nicco pushed back memories of another reporter with the same tenacity and shook his head to clear the images that had taken up residence there. He had a client to protect. It was one thing to bring up a bittersweet memory, another to let it interfere with his ability to do the job.

He noticed that she was rubbing her right arm. "Did I hurt you?"

"Are you kidding? You saved my life."

"You think the shot was meant for you?" Nicco already knew she was a target, but he was interested in her response.

Her face blanked of all expression.

"I really don't know."

He watched as Scout walked away, and after making sure that she was all right, he headed to the balcony, zeroed in on the detective in charge, and identified himself. "Nicco Santonni with S&J Security/Protection, assigned to Scout McAdams. She doesn't know I was hired to protect her, and I'd just as soon keep it that way for as long as I can."

"Gotcha."

Whenever possible, S&J tried to play nice with law enforcement. It made things easier for both sides.

"Wagner," the man said and ignored Nicco's outstretched hand. He pointed to the weapon the shooter had left behind. "Probably didn't want to take the time to break it down and carry it out of here. The number's been filed off, though we've had pretty good success with raising numbers in the past using an acid wash."

Nicco moved closer. "An M110, Knight's Armament semiautomatic with a bipod. Effective range 800 meters."

Wagner looked impressed. "You know your weapons."

"You could say that. Rangers. Six years in the

Stand," Nicco said, using the military's slang for Afghanistan.

The detective gave a low whistle. "Not too shabby." He tapped his chest. "Marine Force Recon. Eight in Fallujah." He gestured to his right leg. "Took a round in my thigh. Still aches in the rain." He grimaced. "I'd give anything to be back fighting the good fight."

Nicco felt a thaw in the air. "Know what you mean."

The two men regarded each other with fresh respect.

"Glad to have you on board," Wagner said and this time held out his hand.

Nicco took the detective's hand, found it ridged with calluses. "Thanks." He inspected the weapon further. "This bad boy's military issue. A very nice and very expensive toy."

"Some toy." Wagner eyed Nicco with a shrewd gaze. "You think your client was the intended victim."

"Had to be," Nicco said frankly, wincing when he thought of just how close the shots had come to Scout. "She's been receiving threats." Curiosity over the reporter buzzed in his head like an insistent gnat.

"She neglected to tell me that." Wagner scowled. "Reporters are a pain..." He bit off whatever he'd been about to add.

Nicco grinned. "Tell me about it."

In perfect accord, they fixed their gazes once more on the weapon. It was the only lead they had to the shooter.

Nicco had been facetious when he'd referred to it as a toy. It was a serious weapon intended to kill with cold and ruthless efficiency.

Whoever wanted Scout McAdams dead was playing for keeps. It was up to him to make sure they didn't succeed.

TWO

Scout woke up sick to her stomach. Her skin was clammy, her heart racing as though she'd just finished a marathon. Invisible hands tightened around her throat, constricting her ability to breathe. Salt rimmed her skin where she'd sweated through her nightshirt.

Gently, she massaged her neck, trying to loosen the bands that were closing in with every second and prevent an attack that would leave her gasping for air. The effort to breathe had turned her mouth cottony, and she swallowed in a vain attempt to rid herself of the dryness.

She'd thrashed through the night, unable to suck in sufficient air, gasping hoarsely as she fought off unseen assailants. In the end, the bad guys won.

They always did.

Not last night, she thought. The good guys, in the form of one very appealing man, had saved the day. Nicco Santonni. She tasted the words on her lips, found them intriguing and surprisingly sweet.

Enough. She had a job to do, one which didn't include mooning over last night's rescuer, no matter how ruggedly handsome he was.

Not even the memory of the good-looking man, however, could banish the aftereffects of the nightmare, including the sensation that she was choking. She swallowed harshly in an attempt to combat it.

It had been a month since she'd had the nightmare but it had returned last night. With a vengeance. Bitter bile rose in her throat. She willed it down.

Breathe.

In.

Out.

She repeated the breathing exercises, slowly inhaling and exhaling, until she could feel the terrifying panic subside. *You're okay.* Her therapist's voice slid into her mind.

I'm okay. She repeated the words until she started to believe them.

Scout turned to her side where she could gaze at the picture of her parents and herself on the day of her graduation from college. *We were all so happy.* Four years after the picture had been taken, her world had shattered into pieces and she was left alone.

The memory of the night her parents had been murdered a scant year ago pierced her heart, a lethally-tipped arrow that never failed to hit its mark. Someday, maybe, the pain would lessen, but it remained as poisonous as ever. She squeezed back tears of frustration and anger.

When was she going to be able to put the attack behind her, those toxic reminders that she wasn't normal? They had burrowed under her skin and into her heart with a tenacity that wouldn't be shaken. She'd dealt with them before. She'd do it again, but, oh, how she wished she didn't have to.

Prayer was her first and best defense. *Lord, I need Your help. I can't do it on my own. I know that You and You alone have the power to heal me. I give myself into Your hands.*

Within seconds, His love washed over her, and the panic slowly edged away. The Lord had not yet banished the nightmares, but He had given her the precious gift of peace when the memories threatened to overwhelm her.

Gratitude for His goodness filled her, replacing the pain with an acceptance that He worked on His timetable, not hers. Impatient by nature, she needed the occasional reminder of His eternal plan and His wisdom.

When the worst of the nausea was under control, she started to get up. Stopped. Big mistake. She hurt all over. Being thrown to the floor by a drop-dead-gorgeous man may make for good fiction, but the reality was less fun than what romance novels made it out to be. Maybe the pain would take her mind off the nightmare and the memories it had engendered.

She took a minute, another, before trying to move again. Cautiously, she pushed herself into a sitting position, paused, lifted one leg over the side of the bed, then the other.

When the room stopped spinning, she stood. Assessed. So far, so good. Every fiber of her body ached, but at least she was moving. Sort of. She hobbled to the full-length mirror attached to the back of her bedroom door and surveyed herself.

Her second mistake of the morning.

Bruises bloomed along her shoulders and arms. Angry red now, they'd soon turn blue and purple, then a sickly green and finally a putrid yellow. It could have been worse. She could have a bullet lodged in her shoulder. Or her heart.

Thanks to the quick actions of Nicco Santonni, she was in one piece. More or less.

Her sense of humor got a toehold, nudging a smile out of hiding. Maybe she'd put in for medical leave. At least it would get her out of covering the month of events leading up to the huge ball where Patrice Newtown, the undisputed queen of Savannah society, would present the mayor with a check large enough to build a new shelter for the city's homeless.

For reasons of her own, Newtown had requested that Scout be assigned to cover a bunch of boring social events. The order had come from the big man himself, Gerald Daniels, the paper's publisher.

Scout was fighting her way onto the paper's crime beat one column inch at a time, and, because of a whim of one of the city's so-called benefactors, she was now relegated once more to the society page. She had as much interest in society doings as she did in learning how to peel an artichoke. Who cared which designer created the dress the mayor's wife wore to the country club dance or what entrée was served with what wine?

Gingerly, she made her way to the shower, where the hot water temporarily soothed her aches and pains and allowed her to forget, for a few minutes at least, the reason for them. Though she normally skipped makeup, she applied a light dusting of blush and mascara and dabbed concealer beneath her eyes. A critical look at herself in the mirror confirmed what she already knew. She couldn't erase the shadows under her eyes or the tiny tension lines that bracketed her mouth.

She braced her hands on the bathroom counter, then dropped her gaze to her splayed fingers, staring at them as though they held the secrets to all the world's questions, but there were no answers there. Within a half hour, she was dressed and out the door, albeit at a slower pace than normal.

After graduating from college and starting at the paper, she promised herself she'd search for the truth. Finding that truth, wherever it lay, had been her compass for the last five years. That quest had taken on special significance with the murder of her parents a year ago. She'd vowed then to find the truth behind the murders and bring down those responsible.

At the office, she did a fast read of her emails, deleted most of them and prepared to write the piece on last night's gala while the events were still fresh in her mind. Not the warm-fuzzy piece Newtown had probably expected, but, hey, publicity was publicity. Then she planned on tracking down Leonard Crane.

She tuned out the chatter of computers, the good-natured ribbing that went on between colleagues, and the constant grumbling about the swill that passed for coffee and concentrated on writing the piece. An hour later, she read it, decided it would do and pushed the Send key.

"McAdams, special delivery." The office gofer handed her a large envelope with no return address. Cold brushed the back of her neck as she noted that it was identical to the other letters.

"Thanks." Scout signed for it, slit open the envelope and looked at the message composed with words cut from a magazine and pasted on a sheet of cheap paper. Another threat. Okay. She'd dealt with threats ever since she'd earned her first byline in the paper's city section.

This was no different.

She read the words aloud, testing them. "Mind your own business. Or we'll mind it for you." She pinched her lips together even as she shook her head, as though the slight movement would dispel the unwanted picture the letter etched in her mind.

Scout prided herself on her independence and self-reliance, but right now she wished she had someone to stand with her.

She'd thought she'd found that with her ex-fiancé, Bradley Middleton, but, after wooing her and even asking her to marry him, he'd left her. The experience had soured her on men for the moment. Maybe forever.

Forget Bradley and concentrate on the letter. Only, she didn't want to think about the letters she'd received over the last month. She had never been one to stick her head in the sand, so why was she doing just that with the letters that were coming with increasing regularity? Nothing she'd done lately was like her, including wasting time thinking about Nicco Santonni.

Now that she wasn't so shaken from nearly getting killed, she'd put it together. Nicco Santonni. Brother to Sal Santonni, her best friend Olivia's husband.

It didn't take much to call up a picture of her rescuer in her mind. Inky black hair a little too long for current fashion, ebony eyes hooded beneath slashing brows and sharply angled cheekbones made for an arresting face. Add to that a body that looked like it was forged from steel and you had a man whom any woman would stop and give a second…or third glance to.

She forced her thoughts away from the handsome Nicco Santonni to her self-imposed mission. Digging into union murders meant investigating the unions themselves. When her mother had begun research for her exposé of Savannah's labor unions, she'd told Scout that graft was most often the cause of murder in unions. Ironically, that same research had resulted in the murder of both of Scout's parents.

Six weeks ago, Scout had started going through her parents' papers. She should have done it months earlier, but after her release from the hospital, she'd been too bogged down in grief and pain to look through their belongings. She'd started with her father's notes for the university physics classes he taught. The clutter triggered a memory of his self-deprecatory comparison to

Disney's absentminded professor. He was a brilliant lecturer but chronically disorganized in his paperwork.

With a sigh, she'd turned her attention to her mother's research for her latest true-crime book. It was among those notes that Scout had found information about Leonard Crane and her mother's belief that he was involved with union murders.

For the last six weeks, Scout had been digging for proof behind her mother's suspicions. Not for the first time, she wished she had plunged into the investigation earlier.

She'd healed from her bullet wound far more quickly than she had the crippling pain of acknowledging that her parents had been taken from her through a hideous act of violence. After leaving the hospital, she'd wandered around in a daze for months. It was only recently that she'd been able to set aside her grief to fix her attention on finding the truth.

She wadded the paper into a ball and then executed a perfect three-pointer into the trash can. Upon reflection, she stood, walked to the trash can, and retrieved the paper.

Why had this threat turned her into a Nervous Nellie? Scout forced a laugh over her uncharacteristic fears. That wasn't who she was.

Her hometown was a beautiful city, steeped in history and tradition, but it wasn't without its faults. She had seen firsthand the ugliness that lay beneath the beauty, the violence that destroyed lives and occasionally even took them.

The crumpled paper in her hand yanked her back to the present.

Meticulously, she smoothed the creases from the paper, and glanced at the message once more. Scout didn't intend on giving up her investigation. Some accused her of being stubborn. She preferred to see it as determination, the same determination that had fueled her ambition to expose the dark secrets of the city since the night she'd lost her parents.

The aftereffects of the nightmare dogged her throughout the day, following her around like a shadow. Much as she tried to shake the feelings, they clung to her like a burr.

After prayer, work was her antidote against the pain.

When her cell phone chirped, she glanced at the number, saw it was blocked. More than once she'd received blocked calls which had ended up giving her valuable information. She picked it up, heard a mechanically altered voice.

"If you want to get the goods on Crane, be at the docks at three fifteen." The voice went on to give directions as to where she should stand if she wanted to see Crane taking a bribe.

Common sense told her to ignore the tip, which

could be a setup, but she couldn't. She wished she had someone who'd go with her, and her thoughts took her back to Nicco Santonni.

Unwillingly, she acknowledged that he had stirred something in her, an attraction she hadn't felt in too long, not since her fiancé, a reporter at a local TV station, had dumped her.

Impatient with herself, she pushed Bradley out of her thoughts. She'd already wasted enough time and tears on him. She had more important things to think about.

Like who wanted her dead.

A relief agent had taken over the detail last night when Scout McAdams had left the ball-room. Though Nicco was primary in the protection unit, no one operative could effectively guard a client twenty-four seven. Usually operatives worked in threes, eight hours on, sixteen off. Because Olivia had asked for Nicco specifically, he'd opted for twelve-hour shifts.

He'd clocked seven hours sack time and had spent the other five finishing the paperwork for which his boss and friend Shelley Judd was a stickler.

"Trying to get on my good side?" Shelley asked when he turned in the expense report she'd been nagging him about for the last two days.

Since S&J had opened an office in Savannah

last year, Shelley spent a couple of days there every month. With the arrival of baby Chloe, Shelley didn't get out in the field as often as she'd like, but she still knew every operation and every assignment.

Nicco smiled at the picture of his hard-hitting boss in her role as mother. Shelley Rabb Judd and brother Jake Rabb, co-founders of S&J, had never known a loving mother's care. Nicco knew she gave her child everything she'd been denied, most of all love.

The once efficiently streamlined office now resembled a nursery with a bassinet and other baby items spilling over the space. Six-month-old Chloe had definitely made her appearance known.

"Always." He bent to brush a kiss over the downy hair of the baby nestled at Shelley's shoulder. "Motherhood suits you."

Dimples peeked out in her pixie face. "I'm operating on three hours' sleep. My shirt has spit-up on it. I haven't had a decent haircut or a manicure since before Chloe was born. And I couldn't be happier."

"I'm glad. For you and for Caleb."

Shelley and ex-Delta Caleb Judd had endured more than their share of hardship, but they had come out the other side stronger and more in love than ever. Nicco knew a moment of envy for what they shared.

"Thanks. When it happens for you, you'll think you've been hit by a semi and then you'll wonder how you lived without that special someone in your life for as long as you did."

Nicco summoned a smile he was far from feeling. He'd already met the *special someone* Shelley spoke of and she'd died. Happily-ever-after wasn't in the future for him. Not any longer.

Unwilling to prolong that topic, he turned the subject to his current assignment. As Shelley was friends with Scout, he knew his boss would have a special interest in the job. He filled her in on the little he knew so far.

"I know Scout's in good hands," Shelley said. "I also know she won't make it easy for you to protect her."

"I'll make it work."

"You always do."

"Got to go." He pecked Shelley's cheek.

He had just enough time for a visit to the police station before he was back on duty. At the station, he asked for Detective Wagner and was directed to a cubbyhole of an office.

Upon seeing Nicco, Wagner stood, held out his hand. "Santonni."

The men shook hands briefly.

"I stopped by to see if you'd learned anything from the weapon from last night," Nicco said.

"Not from the weapon itself, but ballistics traced the trajectory of the shot and found that it was sighted on Ms. McAdams. If you hadn't pushed her to the floor..." The detective let the rest of the sentence go unfinished.

They spent a few more minutes kicking around theories before Nicco checked his watch. He had to be back on duty in less than thirty minutes. "Thanks. If you find out anything, I'd appreciate a heads-up."

"Same goes."

He met another S&J operative outside Scout's office for the handoff. The agent looked over Nicco's shoulder. "She's heading this way."

Scout paused, lifting her head as though sensing something. Fortunately, Nicco knew how to blend in with a crowd, and she didn't make him.

He'd seen Scout McAdams in a dark pantsuit when he'd followed her to the courthouse where she'd gone to cover a story two days ago. Last night, he'd seen her in an evening gown. But this was the first time he'd seen her in jeans and a white T-shirt, with her hair pulled back in a simple ponytail.

She looked smaller, somehow, and younger. More fragile. He doubted she'd appreciate the description. Everything he'd learned about the reporter told him that she was independent to a fault and prided herself on being able to handle anything.

Look at how she'd reacted last night: she hadn't fallen apart when shot at, and, in fact, had tried to comfort others. The lady was pure steel, but that didn't mean she was invincible. He settled down to the routine of making himself invisible.

The trick was to not try too hard. Fortunately, Nicco had had years of experience blending into the background, first in the mountain villages of Afghanistan for the Rangers, and now in the far more civilized streets of his hometown.

He'd protect her, whether she knew it or not.

She was being followed.

Scout felt it as surely as she felt the early afternoon sun warm the back of her neck. She didn't turn around to see who was tailing her. Instead of heading directly to her car as she'd intended, she walked to a coffee shop, deliberately taking her time. Every few minutes, she paused, pretending to gaze into a window. No one jumped into a doorway or suddenly pulled out a newspaper to cover his face.

At the coffee shop, she ordered her coffee, black. Fancy coffee drinks baffled her. If all you wanted was a shot of sugar, there were easier—and cheaper—ways to get it. She nursed the coffee as she made her way to her car. After she climbed inside, she took advantage of adjusting her rearview mirror to scan the sidewalk behind her.

Had she imagined it? She couldn't detect anyone tailing her, but she couldn't shake the feeling that she was under surveillance.

She was new to the cloak-and-dagger business. Okay. Play it cool. She kept an eye out as she drove to the docks. Either her tail was really good, or he'd peeled off.

At the docks, she parked her car and walked to the spot the caller had told her was the best vantage point to witness the goings-on of the dock in question. A quick glance around told her that she was not alone. She glanced up at workmen on scaffolding above her hiding spot as they struggled to balance a replacement panel to a warehouse that looked like it should have been condemned during the Carter administration.

The clanging of steel beams grated along her nerves; the smell—a brew of garbage and fish—had her taking shallow breaths through her mouth.

Scout remained where she was and hoped the men didn't spot her. The grumbling and muttering coming from them told her they were fully occupied with their task and not at all concerned with her.

Still, she didn't like the vibe she was getting. An anonymous call that Leonard Crane would be at a certain dock receiving a payoff was too good to pass up.

The docks were controlled by the mob. Organized crime had its hand in everything that passed in and out of Savannah's port, one of the busiest in the United States. No one moved anything without it being approved by the mob bosses.

City fathers made noises about cleaning up the docks and surrounding area. Speeches were given. Raids were staged. And nothing changed. Those in charge maintained that they had done everything possible to end the corruption. And those who had their nose to the street, as Scout did, knew differently. The mob had infiltrated every area of government, from the mayor's office to the police, making any effort to wipe out the corruption impossible.

Crane didn't arrive at the time she'd been given. She wasn't surprised. If he was connected to the murders, he'd be understandably cautious. The pep talk delivered, she should have felt better, but the uneasiness persisted.

The hair at the nape of her neck hackled. Warily, she looked about but didn't see anything to cause the sensation. Despite that, she couldn't shake the inkling of danger. Over the years, she'd learned to pay attention to such impressions.

The clank of metal against metal ratcheted up the tension building inside her as though she had a crank attached to her, tightening every nerve notch by notch.

Crane and another man showed up at that moment. From their angry gestures, they appeared to be arguing.

Abruptly, the men stopped talking and now seemed to be waiting. If she could only get closer...but she didn't want to give away her location. A big part of a reporter's work involved waiting and watching. In many ways, it was like a cop's job. She had friends on the force who reported that boredom was often more deadly than any threat of gunfire.

A rumbling sound alerted her. Before she could move, muscular arms pushed her aside, and a large body fell on top of her, shielding her.

The scaffolding she'd noted earlier tumbled to the ground. If she'd been where she was only a moment ago, she'd have been crushed beneath its weight. Shock rendered her unable to function. Her mouth went dry, her limbs stiff. She couldn't make her legs work.

Strong hands reached down to pull her to her feet. "We've got to stop meeting like this."

Nicco Santonni. "You saved my life. Again."

THREE

Nicco called the police and asked for Wagner, though he didn't expect the detective to find anything more than he had.

Within ten minutes, Wagner showed up. After examining the scene, he shook his head. "You were right. Nothing to indicate it was anything but an accident. But you don't think so." He didn't make it a question, and Nicco didn't treat it as such.

"I don't believe in coincidences," he said. "First, she's targeted last night, then a pile of scaffolding barely misses her today. You do the math."

"I get what you're saying, but there's no proof that today was anything more than an accident." Wagner held up a hand to forestall Nicco's objections. He turned to Scout. "What do you have to say about it, Ms. McAdams?"

"I… I don't know." Her eyes remained cool, her expression neutral, but Nicco noted the clenching and unclenching of her hands. Fear always found an outlet, as did adrenaline.

He felt it coursing through his bloodstream as well, his heartbeat at double-time as he processed the near miss.

"What were you doing here?" Wagner asked.

"I received a tip."

"Care to share?"

She shook her head. "Reporter's privilege."

Wagner scowled but didn't press the matter. "If you—either of you—think of anything, you know where to find me." After slanting one last glance at Scout, he took off.

Nicco was more concerned about Scout than he'd let on. Though the day was unseasonably hot, even for a Georgia summer, she shivered. Reaction. The lady had nearly been reduced to a bug-splat on the ground beneath thousands of pounds of processed wood and metal. That came on the heels of last night's shooting. "You okay?"

"Yeah." She brushed herself off. He watched as she pulled herself together, her shoulders squaring as though bracing for another blow. "Did you tail me here?"

He raised a brow. "What? No thank-you?"

"Sorry. My manners tend to go MIA when I'm almost killed for the second time in two days."

He gave her kudos for a quick recovery. A lot

of people would have gone into hysterics after what she'd barely escaped. "I get that."

"Thank you." The words weren't fancy, but he heard the sincerity behind them. "Thank you for showing up when you did."

Scout looked about, visibly shuddering when her gaze landed on the scaffolding, now scattered like giant pickup sticks over the ground.

Nicco took her arm and tucked her against him, her softer build fitting into the harder planes of his own. "Let's get out of here." They'd come back for her car when she was no longer suffering from shock.

"You don't have to ask twice."

He steered her to his truck. Halfway there, she shrugged off the supporting arm he'd kept around her and marched forward, as though keeping moving was the secret to maintaining control.

He gave her a boost into the truck. "You're no bigger than a minute."

"You know the saying. 'Good things come in small packages.'"

"I know of a little place not far from here. I don't know if you're hungry, but rescuing damsels in distress tends to make me work up an appetite."

She grinned. "I'm hungry enough to forgive that 'damsel in distress' remark, so you're on."

He shut the door and rounded the truck. After

getting in and buckling his seat belt, he turned to her. "Ordinarily, I'd canvass the area, see if anybody saw anything. But this was a setup through and through. I don't think we're going to learn anything. Not here. Not now."

She gave another shiver. "Frankly, the sooner we get out of here, the better."

"You got it."

The restaurant, barely more than an abbreviated alley in size, was packed. Diners crowded at the counter. Nicco apparently knew the owner, for a large man in an apron that might once have been white greeted them with a smile and a "Hiya, Nicco."

"Same to you, Phil. You got room for us?"

"For you, Nicco, anything."

He showed them to a booth. The red vinyl seats and gray Formica counter appeared to be circa 1960s.

Scout didn't have to think about what she wanted. "A double cheeseburger. Extra-large fries. Chocolate shake. And three chocolate chip cookies."

"And a heart-attack chaser on the side," Nicco added with a wry smile.

"You have a problem with my order?"

"No problem. I'm just wondering how someone

your size puts away all that food." His eyebrow hiked. "Or maybe it's just for show."

She made a face at him. "Give me twenty minutes and then be prepared to eat your words."

A fresh-faced waitress, who must have been all of seventeen, showed up to take their order. She never took her eyes from Nicco.

He gave their order to the girl, who giggled and batted her eyelashes at him.

When she left, Scout lifted a brow. "The famous Santonni charm. It's an education to see it in action." She was talking too much. Too fast. A cover for the nerves that skimmed just below the surface.

The banter felt good, a reminder that she was alive. If not for Nicco Santonni, things could have turned out differently.

She owed him. Again. "You've saved my life. Twice."

Nicco didn't say anything, only waited.

The pieces clicked into place. Scout had confided in her best friend Olivia Hammond Santonni about the threatening letters she'd been receiving. Olivia had hired Nicco, her brother-in-law, to protect Scout. It wasn't a coincidence that Nicco had been at the right place at the right time both last night and today.

"Olivia." There was both affection and resignation in the four syllables. Olivia was a great friend, but she fretted over Scout like a mother hen over her chicks.

Nicco nodded. "Got it in one. She's worried about you."

"Look, I appreciate what you've done, but I can take care of myself. I don't need a bodyguard."

"No?"

"No." She let the single word stand. "Consider yourself fired."

"You didn't hire me, so you can't fire me." His maddening logic stymied her. "Olivia would have my hide if something happened to you. According to her, you've been receiving some pretty nasty letters."

At mention of the letters, bands of cold wrapped around Scout's chest, making her wonder if she were having a heart attack. Of course, she wasn't. If she was struggling to catch her breath, well, that was only natural under the circumstances.

A shiver danced down her arms, a delayed reaction to the near-death experience. *Breathe.* The silent reminder had her inhaling quietly, letting the air out slowly. Her mouth had gone so dry at the idea that someone had made a second attempt on her life in less than twenty-four hours that she couldn't even work up enough spit to swallow.

Nicco pushed a glass of water her way. "Drink."

She picked up the glass, held it with trembling

hands, brought it to her mouth. A long sip allowed her to wet her lips.

Bars of sunlight slanted through ancient blinds. She basked in the warmth and felt some of the chill leave her.

He was talking, and she worked to listen to the low rumble of his voice. "You said a tip brought you to the docks?"

Knowing where this was going, she nodded reluctantly.

"Anonymous?"

"Yeah."

He raised his brow, whether at her stupidity for following what was obviously a bogus tip or at her one-word answer, she didn't know.

Another chill shivered through her as she accepted what might have happened if not for Nicco. She hoped he didn't notice anything amiss. He'd probably never known a moment of panic in his life. He had a reassuring way about him, his calm, measured tones like the practiced strides of the soldier Olivia had told her he'd been. His presence made her feel safe, and she could really use a feeling of safety right about now.

Honesty forced her to admit that it wasn't only the attempt on her life that had sent a rush of sensation skittering along her nerves. A tiny thrill had whispered through her when Nicco Santonni pulled her from harm's way. It reminded her of the energy-charged air before a lightning storm struck.

She wanted to believe that the feelings were due to the heightened emotion of the moment, but that was a lie.

"I was following you." His words confirmed her earlier suspicions. He studied her. "You're not as cool as you're pretending. Even hotshot reporters are allowed to have a *moment* after almost being crushed by a couple of tons of steel and wood."

Unwilling to pursue the subject of her reaction to the scaffolding nearly killing her, she turned the tables on him. She made no secret of her scrutiny of him, her gaze shrewd and assessing. Last night, he'd been debonairly handsome in a tux.

Today, with cords of well-toned muscle showing to advantage in a gray T-shirt and black jeans, he was even more devastating.

Though not movie-star handsome, he possessed something more basic: raw power. A combination of roughly drawn features, muscular shoulders and a long, lean build imbued him with a presence that made him hard—make that impossible—to forget.

She tore her gaze away from his chest and lifted it to meet his. He scraped a hand over his cheek, drawing her attention to the dark stubble that shadowed his jaw.

He wasn't as tall or as big as his brother Sal, but there was an inner strength to him, a steely resolve in his eyes. It was that determination that set him apart from other men and put him at the top of the food chain, an apex predator.

Dark eyes were filled with amusement. "You're staring. What's the verdict?"

"You left the military but still have a side of hero complex. You're self-confident but not arrogant. You pride yourself on doing the right thing no matter the cost."

"Not bad."

"Not bad or spot on?" she challenged.

"Not bad. Take it or leave it. Tell me what you know about last night."

"I don't *know* anything."

"What does your gut tell you?"

She put down the menu and sat back, unwilling to share the jumble of feelings that made her stomach feel like it was coated with acid. "Right now it's telling me that I'm hungry. I went off without breakfast and worked through lunch. You want something from me, you need to feed me first."

The food arrived, rich and plentiful, redolent with the smells of grilled meat and fried onions.

She closed her eyes. The silent prayer over the food was both comforting and humbling.

When she looked up, it was to find Nicco watching her keenly. "You were praying, weren't you?"

Her nod was brief. "I'm sorry if it made you uncomfortable." At one time, she'd questioned the idea of praying, even silently, in a public place, but had decided she couldn't worry over the opinions of others. Prayer was an important part of her life. Offering gratitude to the Lord was her way of acknowledging His hand in her life.

"Don't apologize. It was...nice." His gaze dropped. "My family always prayed at meals when I was a kid."

"And now?"

"My parents and sisters still do." He paused. "And Sal."

"And you?"

"I sort of got out of the habit." He popped a French fry into his mouth. "It's good that you do."

"You can, too. God doesn't turn away prayers." She smiled gently. "No matter how rusty they are."

"I'm afraid mine are more than rusty. It's hard to pray when you no longer believe."

"What made you stop?"

"Stuff." He left it at that.

The roughness of his voice told her to back off. She lifted her burger, brought it to her lips, and took a large bite. The meat was grilled to perfection. "Why didn't I know about this place? I thought I knew all the good burger joints."

"Phil—the owner—likes to keep it under wraps. He always says that if it caught on, he'd be busier than he wants."

"He's right." She took another bite and sighed her pleasure.

"How'd you come to be named Scout?"

"My mother taught English at the university before she left to start writing. She did her dissertation on Harper Lee."

"Got it. You're named after the little girl in *To Kill a Mockingbird*."

"Right. Daddy wanted me to go by my grandmother's name—Rachel—but Scout stuck."

"It fits."

She felt Nicco's gaze on her, evaluating, like he was trying to decide whether or not to ask her something. "What've you gotten yourself into?"

She hesitated. Sharing a story before she had all the facts was trouble. More, it smacked of unprofessionalism.

"I'm not out to scoop you."

"As if." Scout did some evaluating of her own. Could she trust him? She'd honed her people-reading skills over the last years, gauging motives and intent by paying attention to body language, facial expressions, and a host of other tells.

Frustration hardened the bodyguard's sun-weathered face, but she didn't detect any hint of deceit in him. His gaze met hers straight on with the precision of a laser. Nicco Santonni might try to steamroll over her, but he wouldn't lie.

When the last fry was consumed and the chocolate shake and cookies only a memory, she gestured to a trash can that was only a few feet away. "You wanted to know why someone's trying to kill me."

"It crossed my mind."

"It has to do with that."

He followed her gaze. "Trash?"

"Trash. Or, if you want to be more precise, garbage."

Twin furrows creased his brow before he nodded in understanding. "The garbage/sanitation industry. That's why you were trying to get to Crane last night."

"Nailed it. Crane's a big name in the unions and I'm investigating union murders." Honesty forced her to add, "Unofficially."

"If it's unofficial, why don't you drop it? Whoever tried to kill you is playing for keeps."

"So am I." She swallowed back frustration at having someone tell her to drop the investigation. "Crane's as slippery as they come. So far he's blocked every effort I've made to talk with him." She brought her fingers together, leaving only a tiny space between them. "I was this close last night to talking with him when..."

"Someone decided to use you for target practice."

"Yeah. That. Thanks for the meal." She stood. "If you don't mind, I need to get my car and head back to work."

"Sure."

He helped her into the truck. At his touch, a zing of awareness raced through her.

Scout turned to him as he steered the truck back to the docks. Pulses of energy flared between the two of them as their gazes connected, jangling her senses. "Seriously, thank you. I wouldn't be here if it wasn't for you."

"Seriously, you're welcome."

Like most reporters, she was a quick study when it came to people. Nicco Santonni appealed to her on a gut-deep level, making her think of toughness and staying power. She made a decision. "If you have time, maybe you can follow me back to the office. There's something I want to show you."

At her office, Nicco read the letter, then reread it. His lips tightened with every word. No doubt about it, the lady was being threatened. He had no use for those who hid behind the cloak of anonymity. Cowards, the lot of them. "The creep went old school," he said, gesturing to the words cut out from a magazine. "Cute."

"Real cute."

The hum of computers, the bustle of bodies on the move, and the scrape of chairs sliding across the linoleum floor filled the oversize room. Overlaying it was a sense of urgency, fed by caffeine and adrenaline. The atmosphere was one of purpose.

A television reporter had been embedded in Nicco's last unit in Afghanistan. Against his better judgment, he'd fallen for her. In a big way. It had been a time of whispered exchanges, soft laughter, stolen kisses. They'd begun talking about the future. A home. Children. When an IED had exploded, killing her and two of his men, he'd nearly gone crazy with grief, blaming himself for failing to keep her safe. Shortly after that, he'd resigned his commission. How could he trust himself when he'd allowed the woman he loved to be killed?

Forcibly, he dragged his thoughts from the past. Scout had nothing to do with the incident that had cost the woman he'd loved her life. With that in mind, he turned his attention to how he could help. "Tell me about the other letters."

"They weren't bad," she said, the reluctance in her tone telling him that there was more to come. "At least, not at first. More like a bully's taunts."

"Let me guess. They got worse."

"Yeah. You could say that."

"How many more?"

"Five." The reluctance grew more pronounced. She dug through a drawer and pulled out the other letters. Her hand shook as she gave them to him. Her flush revealed her embarrassment at the betraying tremor.

He pretended he hadn't noticed. "You're right to be scared. You'd be a fool if you weren't."

She thrust out her chin. "I'm not scared. And I don't run." Her chin hitched another notch, the defiant gesture drawing his attention to the resolute set of her shoulders, the graceful contour of her neck. From there, his gaze dropped to her small but capable hands, the nails unpolished, the fingers unadorned by rings.

With hair that appeared more red than gold in the daylight, a sprinkling of cinnamon freckles and fair skin, she should have looked delicate, soft even. Instead, there was an intensity to her that caused him to forget that she stood barely over five feet and probably didn't weigh more than a buck five. The passion in her eyes when she talked about her work made her appear bigger than she was.

"I took this job to make a difference in the world. This story is personal, but nothing else has changed. I'm still trying to make a difference."

Hadn't he said the same thing when he'd enlisted and again when he'd joined the Rangers? That he wanted to make a difference? Maybe he and Scout were more alike than he'd thought. He regarded her with new insight, saw the truth and sincerity that shone from her eyes.

Her straightforward approach to life was refreshing, yet there was a wariness about her, as though she was on guard against some danger he hadn't identified, one that superseded even the threats.

"No? Then you're not as smart as you look." She'd seemed plenty scared last night and again at the docks today, but he had sense enough to keep that observation to himself.

He'd never thought she'd turn her back on the story, but he'd wanted to get a read on her. The lady reporter had more than her share of guts if what he sensed about her was true.

"Let's go back to the beginning. When did the letters start?"

"Six weeks ago." Pensively, she pinched the skin between her brows. "I didn't pay much attention when they first started coming. Getting nasty-grams is part of the job."

He doubted she was aware of her fingers kneading the narrow space above her nose. "Around the same time you started poking around union murders?"

"Yeah."

"And you think they're connected to Crane and garbage?" He lifted a brow. "Dirty business."

She rolled her eyes. "Like that's the first time I've heard that."

FOUR

Appreciating her, he returned the grin with one as fast as her own. "I try to be original."

"Try harder."

Okay. Maybe this wouldn't be a total bore. Scout McAdams was quick-witted, with a tongue as sharp as the articles she penned. That didn't mean he was going to roll over on security matters, though.

"We need to establish some ground rules."

"Good. I'll let you know when I need you. Otherwise, stay out of my way." She rose, obviously preparing to leave.

He rose as well. And towered over her. "Ms. McAdams, you've got it all wrong. I set the rules. You follow them. Got it?"

"Mr. Santonni, you're the one who has it wrong," she said, matching his annoyance. "I do as I please, and right now it pleases me to leave. I promised myself a run today. I'm not going to cancel it just because you've decided to hold onto my skirts."

Obviously the lady had forgotten her fear of moments ago when she'd showed him the threatening letter. He didn't want her to live in a state of perpetual panic, but a little healthy fear could be good.

"Fine. We'll go together."

If the mutinous glare she shot him was any indication, they were both in for a roller coaster of a ride.

"I either go with you or you don't go at all." He gave a hard smile. "And, just for the record, it's been a long time since I held onto a woman's skirts. Last time I remember doing it, I was around five years old and the woman was my mother."

Unexpectedly, she smiled with such warmth that he came close to doing a double take. The smile turned him upside down. It was genuine and came really close to being sweet.

"You must love your mother a lot." There was wistfulness in the words, a poignancy that reached down inside of him.

It was true. He loved his mother with all his heart. She'd put up with a lot from him. Not to mention his brother Sal, whom she claimed had turned her hair gray before she was thirty, and their three sisters. Rosa Santonni was a force to be reckoned with and made no apologies for it. "What makes you say that?"

"The way you said 'my mother.' There was so much love in the words." Sadness edged her voice, and he knew she was thinking of her parents. His background check of Scout had turned up the information that her parents had been killed in a carjacking.

"It's true. I love her a great deal. And she'd be the first to tell you that once I take a job, I don't let go until it's finished. The way I see it, you and I are just getting started. You've got some lowlife sending you threats. You need someone to keep you safe until he's put in a cage."

"And you think you're that someone?" Sadness was replaced with tartness. The lady gave as good as she got.

"I was an Army Ranger." For Nicco, that said it all.

He'd always wanted to be part of the kind of brotherhood Sal had found with Delta. At the same time, he'd wanted to make his mark in his own way. He'd found that with the Rangers. Their legendary courage, resourcefulness and integrity resonated within him, and he had dedicated himself to being worthy of that elite group.

He'd found what he was looking for. And more. The men he served with were the best of the best. They gave their all to their unit. Nicco had grown in unexpected ways, finally being assigned to command a unit of his own.

"Fair enough."

She stood, crossed to the window and looked out, a slim figure silhouetted in the afternoon sun.

"I can't stop doing my job just because of a couple threats. I was overreacting. I've had threats in the past. They never amounted to anything."

"But there was something about this one," he guessed, studying her, "that made you stop. Stop and wonder if there was more to it than just empty words."

An unreadable expression crossed her face. "Maybe. For a minute. But I've had time to think it through. It's just the usual, some coward who didn't like something I wrote and decided he'd get cute with a pair of scissors and cut-out words." Her shrug was casual to the extreme, but it didn't quite mask the fear that flickered in her eyes.

Nicco was puzzled until he realized that she was trying to convince herself that she hadn't been the target the night before, and that today's near-miss at the docks had merely been an accident. He understood the need to rationalize away the incidents.

Despite her brave words, it was clear she believed she was in danger. It was equally clear she didn't want his help.

Whether she wanted it or not, he planned on giving it. The lady was in over her head. From what he'd seen of the letters, they'd grown progressively more threatening. In his experience, people who sent threats like that didn't suddenly back off.

He stood. "Let's go. Until we find out who's sending the letters, I'm your shadow."

Annoyance narrowed her eyes. "I don't need a shadow. Or a bodyguard."

"Maybe not. But you're stuck with me. Get used to it."

With Nicco Santonni following her in his truck, Scout headed home and changed into sweats and sneakers.

Despite it being the middle of the workday, she needed a run to sweat out the fear and tension of the last twenty-four hours. Her editor didn't demand that his people keep a time clock, only that they get their work done. He knew, as did everyone else at the paper, that Scout put in enough extra hours that there was never a question of her shirking her job.

Having a bodyguard tag along beside her wasn't part of the plan, but she accepted that she wasn't going to get rid of him. The part of her brain that wouldn't tolerate a lie admitted that maybe she needed him.

She shot him a challenging look when she found him waiting for her. "You want to stick with me, fine. But I'm going for a run. Come or stay. Your choice."

"I'll try to keep up," he said humbly.

Deciding that didn't deserve a response—the man was clearly in top shape—she started out. She jogged past the strip mall that had stirred up controversy in her neighborhood when the zoning laws had been changed, past the bakery that made the chocolate-filled scones she was quickly becoming addicted to and past the library that had been a second home when she'd been a child.

He kept pace easily. Too easily. He was probably laughing silently at her.

Didn't matter. She wasn't out to impress anyone.

With every step, she felt the tension draining from her, even though she was pushing her body to its limit. The faster she ran, the more she felt her mind clearing. Two attempts on her life within a day's time was daunting, but she refused to allow them to stop her from finding the truth behind her parents' murders.

She *knew* the story her mother had been working on was at the root of everything, including the recent attacks on herself. The story, Georgette McAdams had once told Scout, would rip the city wide open when everything came out. "It'll topple Savannah's unions. Watch and see."

Preoccupied with her own work, Scout hadn't paid much attention at the time. Now she wished she had. Unfortunately, her mother's prediction hadn't come true. She was murdered only two weeks later.

Scout didn't need a psychiatrist to tell her that she was trying to outrun the past. She ran every day, rain, shine, blistering heat or freezing cold. It didn't matter. The slap of her sneakers against the pavement empowered her in a way little else could. She used the familiar rhythm to sort out her thoughts.

Her parents had raised her to be independent. Accepting that she needed help came at a cost. Though she prayed every day, both in gratitude and in seeking the Lord's guidance, asking someone else for help grated against everything she was.

The soft material of her T-shirt blotted the sweat that ran down her neck and chest. She ran faster, determined to outrun the memories that chased her.

With her arms and legs pumping, she kept up a steady pace, her thoughts jogging along with her stride, taking her back to her first day at the paper over five years ago. She'd arrived with piein-the-sky dreams of being the best reporter to ever work at the city's number one newspaper.

Those dreams were quickly knocked back to reality when she was assigned to the obits first, and then the classifieds. She'd refused to be discouraged and dug in with the same perseverance that had enabled her to complete a four-year degree in only three. The work was often mind-numbing, but she'd never lost track of her goal. From the first, she'd set her sights on the crime beat of the city section. No job was too little, too menial for her to do as she rose steadily in the ranks.

Her can-do attitude and consummate professionalism snagged the attention of one editor after another until she'd finally caught the eye of the publisher, Gerald Daniels. He was a hands-on owner who had taken an interest in her and encouraged her to bring stories to him when she felt she was on to something big.

Another mile and she'd be done. Five miles a day enabled her to indulge in the occasional scone and to keep the tension of the job at bay. She was in the best shape of her life—physically. Mentally was another matter.

Her emotions were all over the place. Look at how she'd reacted to Nicco Santonni. The attraction she felt for him gave her pause. After her engagement had ended, she'd made a point of keeping men at a distance. The last thing she needed was a man in her life, no matter how handsome.

Intensely aware of him at her side, she kept her gaze straight ahead, but it was impossible to ignore the steady rhythm of his stride.

Scout wasn't sure why she'd asked him to look at the letters, aside from the gut feeling that he'd give her an honest opinion about them. He was a straight shooter, like his brother.

The chirp of her phone had her reaching for it. Her editor.

"Get to the courthouse steps. Patrice Newtown is giving a press conference in forty-five minutes about the charity ball."

Scout nearly groaned. She was already weary of hearing about the ball which wasn't even scheduled for another couple of weeks.

"I want direct quotes. Grab Tagg," her editor added, naming the paper's photographer.

"Yes, sir." She made an abrupt turn, started back in the opposite direction.

Nicco turned to face her, running backward, never losing a step. "Finished already?"

"Duty calls. The Duchess is holding a press conference outside the courthouse. I'm supposed to cover it."

A frown dug furrows around Nicco's mouth. "Can't they get someone else?"

Now it was her turn to frown. "It's my job."

"Courthouse, here we come."

They raced each other back to her house. "Give me twenty minutes," she called to Nicco as she climbed the stairs to her bedroom. She spared a moment to text the photographer and give him a heads-up.

She showered and dressed in record time and was on her way to the courthouse in the promised twenty minutes.

Nicco drove. "No sense taking two vehicles," he said.

She knew it was more than that. He wanted to stick as close as possible to her. The two of them needed to smooth out the kinks for a working relationship. She had a feeling that Nicco Santonni was accustomed to getting his own way. Well, he'd find that she was just as determined when it came to fighting for what she wanted.

Print and TV journalists crowded the courthouse steps where Patrice Newtown stood. More like holding court, Scout thought, a trifle uncharitably. She prepared herself for a candy-coated speech full of self-aggrandizement and grandiose plans that didn't have a chance of succeeding.

Scout had already dug up background material on the woman. Her husband, Edmund Newtown, had traced his ancestry to several generations before the War of Northern Aggression. In the

South, proving your ancestry was mandatory if you didn't want to be considered an upstart.

Patrice's maiden name was Copperwood. A wedding announcement some thirty years old featured a picture of a young Patrice Copperwood and Edmund Newtown. Best man was listed as Edmund's brother, Charles, and matron of honor Irene Copperwood Kruise.

The last had given Scout pause. Kruise. Something niggled at the back of her mind.

A link to an obituary detailing Edmund's death had taken her to a notice of the dissolution of assets of Newtown Industries. She'd read further and discovered that the Newtowns had been on the verge of bankruptcy when a sudden infusion of cash had replenished the family fortune.

Digging deeper, she'd followed links to various financial journals. No mention was made of where the money had come from. With the death of her husband, Patrice Newtown became the face of the charity he'd started.

Scout shoved everything else from her mind when Newtown began to speak, her voice vibrant with passion in describing the plight of Savannah's homeless.

Scout volunteered at a shelter for teenage girls whenever she found the time and donated whatever money she could spare.

It wasn't enough. It was never enough.

The work was both heartbreaking and rewarding. The stories she heard tore at her heart, all the more so when she realized that all the measures taken by both the city and its charities were at best a bandage on what appeared to be an incurable disease.

"Hey," Tagg said, arriving with the backpack he was never without. "The Duchess summons, and we mere mortals appear."

She grinned at his reference to Newtown as Duchess. The name was commonly used in describing Newtown, who was the closest thing to royalty that Savannah society could boast.

"When will we realize that the problem of homelessness is everyone's problem?" Newtown asked.

As Newtown outlined ideas for the proposed shelter, Scout couldn't help wondering if the words were empty ones. She elbowed her way forward, all the time aware of Nicco. His stance was one of hypervigilance, and she wondered if others were curious about the good-looking man who was no more than a foot away from her at any given time.

"What actions do you propose taking that the city's not already doing?" Scout shouted above other voices. "What makes you think you'll succeed where others haven't?"

All eyes turned first to her, then to Newtown.

The lady took her time in answering. "Good question. I don't have all the answers, but I have committed myself and my charity to wiping out homelessness in our city. Those of you who have visited the shelters know that they are overwhelmed, understaffed and underfunded. That's why I plan to devote the money from the coming months' fund-raising efforts to building a new shelter, one that will accommodate more people, provide education and job-training, and even on-site medical care."

Applause burst through the crowd.

"Money alone won't solve the problem," Scout shouted above the din.

"You're right. Money doesn't solve problems by itself. That's why we need everyone's help." Newtown swept her gaze over the crowd. "I'm challenging each of you to give of your time. Volunteer to read to the children at the shelters. Sort clothing. Serve at the food pantry. Whatever you can do, do it. Together, we'll make a difference."

More applause sounded until Newtown raised her hands. "A gala held in a few weeks will highlight our efforts. Tickets are still available for those who have not yet purchased them. Thank you for coming today. With support like this, I know we'll reach our goal."

Scout found herself responding to the woman's speech with reluctant approval. Socialites like Patrice Newtown weren't on Scout's A-list, but they could accomplish what ordinary people couldn't.

She turned to Tagg. "Did you get enough pictures?"

He tapped his camera. "Sure did. Didn't even need a filter. The lady photographs like a dream."

Rich, compassionate and beautiful. It seemed Patrice Newtown had it all.

Scout directed a smile at Tagg. "Thanks. You're the best."

"Tell that to the boss. My paycheck looked anemic the last time I checked."

She chuckled. "Haven't you heard? Anemic's the new black."

"I'd rather have my checking account *in* the black."

His irrepressible humor tugged a smile from her. Tagg was twenty-three, only three years her junior, but sometimes he seemed impossibly young. Or maybe she was just feeling old. Two attacks in two days could do that to a person. She inhaled deeply, a vain attempt to calm her pulse, which still had an annoying tendency to race when she thought of the last two days.

"Hey, you all right?" he asked, lines of concern marring his smooth brow. "I heard about the shooting last night."

"Fine." The lie tasted sour upon her lips, but she wasn't going to share the fact that she'd been receiving death threats and had had attempts made on her life. That kind of news would circulate through the office at warp speed.

He gave her a doubtful look. "You sure? And who's the big guy who glares at anyone who looks at you twice?"

"He's a friend. He offered to drive me here."

Tagg nodded. "Okay. If you're done with me, I'm going to take off. I want to get these pictures downloaded. I'll go through them, then shoot the best of the bunch to you."

"Thanks again."

"No problem. You make my job easy. You always know just what you want." The warmth in his voice caused her to flush.

More than once, Tagg had hinted that he'd like to ask her out. She'd ignored the hints and had worked to keep their relationship on a professional level.

Nicco kept close, making her hyperaware of his presence. She did her best to ignore him, but that was proving difficult. She was discovering that he was not a man to be easily ignored. He was too big, too male, too overpowering to stay in the background.

Though intensely conscious of her bodyguard's displeasure, Scout didn't rush off, wanting to mill around, gauge the reactions to Newtown's remarks. She learned a great deal by talking with people in the crowd at such events.

She wanted to see what they thought of the speech so she could add some quotes to the story. She smiled her best reporter's smile, the one that invited people to open up. A veteran reporter had taught her the value of "just-between-me-and-you" questions, and while Scout had appreciated the advice, she genuinely wanted to hear the reactions of those who had gathered to hear Newtown's speech.

When the crowd dispersed, she continued to hang around, listening to the other reporters. Journalists had seen it all. They were rarely taken in by pretty words or pretty faces.

Pretending not to notice Nicco's scowl, she zeroed in on a reporter from a competing paper.

"She came off as sincere," he said. "She plays the Lady Bountiful role well, may even mean it."

"Do you think she can pull it off?" Scout asked. "Building a new shelter?"

"I think a woman like that can do anything she sets her mind to." This came from a television reporter. "What did you think of the plug for the lady's big shindig? Like regular Joes can afford the price of one of those tickets."

Scout had wondered the same thing. She'd been given two tickets, one for herself and one for a guest, to cover the event; otherwise, there'd be no way she could have afforded the cost of attendance.

Would Nicco accompany her to the gala? Anticipation sparked within her at the idea of seeing him in evening wear once again. She did her best to squelch it with the stern reminder that he was her bodyguard. Nothing more.

"Time will tell if she wants to help the city or just help herself," the first journalist said.

That snagged Scout's attention. "What do you mean?"

"People with Newtown's money don't do anything unless it helps them. That's a rich people maxim."

"That's pretty cynical." Scout felt compelled to defend Newtown.

"You know what the world's like."

She nodded. More than most, she knew what the world was like. She'd seen firsthand the results of violence. That didn't mean that she'd stopped believing. In people. In the Lord.

"Thanks, guys. See you later." She had a story to write.

Nicco didn't like the open venue. He especially didn't like that Scout refused to stay put. She was all over the place, talking to one reporter, then another. The boy assigned as her photographer shadowed her, but he was no protection. He had the engaging manner of a puppy, eager to please and totally clueless to any impending danger.

Dusk had settled, smudging the sky with a purple gray haze that was more smog than darkness.

Nicco grabbed her elbow. "You've got your story. Let's get out of here."

She frowned. "I've got to go to the office."

It was his turn to frown. "Can't you write from home?"

"Yeah, but—"

"But nothing. I can't protect you here out in the open. And your office is a free-for-all with people coming and going all the time."

"I can't stop doing my job because of some letters." And a couple of attempts on her life. But she didn't add that. Giving voice to the incidents gave them more power, and that she was unwilling to do.

"You were pretty scared earlier."

She opened her mouth, then closed it. "You're right. I was. I have to clear it with my boss." She made a call, explained that she planned to work at home. "Thanks," she said when he agreed and ended the conversation.

Scout was subdued on the drive back to her house. He hadn't meant to shut her down like that, but he had a job to do. Keeping her safe meant controlling the environment. Her home turf was the best place for that.

The pint-size reporter wasn't what he'd expected. She was forthright, honest and, most surprisingly of all, a believer. Most of the journalists he'd met, with the notable exception of Ruth, tended to be hardened and callous, viewing the world through the lens of cynicism. And though Scout wasn't naive, her quiet faith set her apart.

He knew she struggled in accepting his protection. Her independence came through loud and clear in everything she said, everything she did. He respected that, admired it even, but it didn't make it easy to safeguard her.

Nicco had an obligation to not only protect her but to find out who was targeting her. He couldn't get the letter she'd shown him out of his mind.

There were software programs designed to determine in which magazines certain words appeared in a particular font and color, but knowing what magazines were used didn't automatically point to the identity of the sender.

Finding that individual was going to take serious computer skills. He'd leave that to Shelley, who was not only one of S&J's founders but a tech geek bar none as well.

"Okay if I stop at my place for a shower and a change of clothes? I'm pretty sweaty after our run."

"Sure."

He pulled up to the shotgun-style home he'd

bought last year, showed her inside, and looked at it through her eyes. The unfinished construction in the front room where he'd planned to redo the fireplace and wainscoting. The shabby furniture that was a collection of hand-me-downs. The faded wallpaper that was probably fifty years old.

He was taking his time, choosing materials that were true to the era and crafting them to last. His latest project was restoring the hardwood floors to their original condition. The patina of polished oak gleamed softly in the late afternoon light.

"Sorry about the mess."

"Don't apologize. You're taking your time, making it something that says who and what you are."

He hadn't thought of it that way. "Yeah. I am." No one else had recognized or appreciated that. "Thank you."

"For what?"

"For making me see what I'm working for."

"You're a craftsman."

"Hardly." He held up his hands, studied them. "But I like working with my hands."

He watched as her gaze moved around the room. "It shows."

A rush of pleasure filled him at the simple words before he remembered that he had a job to do, a job that didn't involve basking in the warm glow of his client's compliments. "I'll grab a shower and some clothes."

"Take your time. If it's okay, I'll look around."

After a shower and a quick change of clothes, Nicco was driving Scout back to her place. He had a lot to digest. About Scout McAdams. About who wanted her dead. About his unexpected attraction to her. It was the last that caused his lips to tighten.

He wouldn't get involved with a reporter again. He'd already done that once, with disastrous results. Aside from that, Scout was a client. That put her firmly off-limits. A smile tipped the corners of his lips as he thought of two of his co-workers and his brother, all of whom had found love while on the job.

The smile winked out. Love and happy-ever-after weren't in the future for him.

FIVE

"How long have you known Olivia?" Nicco asked over delivery pizza and soda in Scout's kitchen that evening.

She plucked a mushroom off her pizza and chewed it thoughtfully. Her earlier run had done her good, but she'd still been keyed up after the near-miss at the docks. Now, with good food and, she admitted, good company, she felt herself relaxing. "A couple of years. We met at an auto-repair class for women." She tapped her chest. "You are looking at class valedictorian."

Nicco's eyes lit with humor. "Don't tell me. Olivia was salutatorian."

"You got it. It didn't hurt that there were only five of us in the class and one woman dropped out before the end of the semester."

"I'm impressed." He chuckled. "You and Olivia, huh? I'm trying to see it, but the picture won't take hold."

"We called ourselves Mutt and Jeff. But it

works." Her voice warmed. "I'm glad she and Sal found each other again."

"Me, too. Sal's never been happier. They want to start a family right away. Mama's in seventh heaven at the idea of more grandchildren."

Scout smiled, but her thoughts took a melancholy turn. There'd been a time when she'd thought she'd found the right man and that they'd marry and start a family. He'd broken her heart and shattered her trust. Since then, she'd been heart-whole and intended on staying that way. Focusing on her career was safer than giving her heart to a man.

"Sal and Olivia are the perfect couple," she said, pulling her thoughts away from that time. "They deserve to be happy. What about you? Do you want the white-picket-fence-and-bikes-in-the-driveway thing?"

"Not in my future," he said.

"I get it. You like the idea of having a girl in each port." She gave him an appraising glance. "Let me guess. You were BMOC. Big Man on Campus," she explained at his quizzical look. "Captain of the varsity football team. Prom king."

The reddening of his cheeks told her she'd gotten at least part of it right.

"Guilty. Except for the BMOC thing. I played football and dated the prom queen. What about you? Homecoming queen. Head of the cheerleading squad. Voted Girl Most Likely to Succeed."

"Hardly. I was Girl Most Likely to Swallow Her Retainer and Choke on It."

He barked out a laugh. "I find that hard to believe."

"Believe it. I was a nerd with a capital *N*."

"You grew out of it just fine."

Now it was her turn to blush. His words brought a rush of pleasure, but she refused to take them seriously. She leaned forward. "I'll let you in on a little secret. I'm still a nerd. I just grew out of the retainer phase."

Humor lit his eyes. "Good to know."

She felt herself responding to his easy manner. He was charming without trying, funny without being obnoxious. Careful, she cautioned herself. She'd fallen for Bradley without knowing the man beneath the good-looking exterior. She wouldn't make that mistake again.

But Nicco didn't give off any warning signals. He was genuine, an honest-to-goodness American hero. He was funny, his comments insightful, and his observations about people dead-on.

She did her best to banish thoughts of how appealing he'd looked with his dark hair still wet from the shower, or how the snug black T-shirt he wore highlighted his broad shoulders.

Her parents would have liked him. Automatically, she fingered the pendant she was never without. A small gold pencil with a diamond at the tip hung from a thin gold chain. A present from her mother upon Scout's graduation from college.

"Pretty," Nicco said. "Something tells me there's a story behind it."

"There is. My parents gave me a car when I graduated from college, not a new one, but better than the beater I'd been driving. Mama wanted to give me something personal as well." Once more, Scout touched the pencil. "She had a jeweler make this. I've never taken it off."

Thoughts of her parents, their love for her, the vow she'd made to expose the truth about their murders, intruded on her enjoyment of the moment, and she pushed her plate away.

"Not hungry?" he asked.

"I lost my appetite."

Nicco studied her. "You're biting the inside of your cheek because you want to say something and don't know if you should."

"There's something you don't know."

"Now's the time to tell me. Spill it."

"There might be another reason someone wants me out of the way."

He got it. "Your parents."

"How did you know?"

"When Olivia asked me to keep an eye on you,

I did a background check. Same as I'd do on any-one," he said.

Her chin came up. "What did you come up with?"

"Your mother was writing another true-crime book, this one about union murders." The topic of Georgette McAdams's new book wasn't common knowledge, but Nicco must have done some digging. "You're finishing what she started." His lips thinned to a hard line. "Whoever's after you thinks she left you her notes, her research. They're afraid you're getting too close."

"My mother had been receiving threats before she died. The carjacking was too convenient to be random."

"If you're right and you keep asking questions, you could be digging yourself the same grave."

She flinched but held his gaze. "I have to do this."

"You're in way over your head. You've got to see that." Urgency leaked through the words.

Her jaw set. "You have a job to do. So do I." She folded her arms over her chest, hoping he took the hint that the matter was closed.

Nicco must have gotten the message for he turned his gaze to the embroidered plaque on the kitchen wall. *Great moments often catch us unaware—beautifully wrapped in what others may consider a small one.* "I like that."

She followed his gaze. "Thanks. Olivia gave it to me when I moved in."

"What's a great moment in your life?"

She didn't have to think about it. "When I saw my first byline. It was a small thing—like the plaque says—but it was everything to me." She cocked her head. "What about you?"

He didn't hesitate. "Holding my first niece in my arms. I've never felt such pure joy."

"What about children of your own?" It was an extremely personal question, but she couldn't keep the words back.

"Like I said—not in the future for me."

Why not? The words trembled on her lips, but she bit them back. "You never know," she said lightly.

"What about you? Do you want children?"

"A houseful. I always wanted brothers and sisters when I was growing up." Regret wadded up in her throat as she realized that she may never achieve this dream. How could she have a family when she couldn't trust men? "I love your big family." She'd met the Santonnis, minus Nicco, at Olivia and Sal's wedding and had been immediately charmed by them.

Only later had she learned that Nicco had been called back to Afghanistan to help teach the defusing of explosives to new members of his unit.

His smile was wry. "It's not all that it's cracked up to be. Always waiting for the bathroom comes to mind."

"You wouldn't trade them for the world." A knot of longing bordering on envy lodged in her throat. The Santonni family was everything she'd dreamed. Once again, she was forced to acknowledge that she may never have that for herself.

"You're right. We're big, loud, and everybody talks over everyone else."

"It's wonderful." Her sigh was wistful.

"That's one way of describing it."

"For me, family means love. 'Eternity is where true love exists.' That's what my father had engraved on my mother's wedding ring." Her voice broke a little. "They were so much in love. Sometimes, when I'm missing them, I think of that and it makes it hurt a little less to know that they're together." Tears gathered in her eyes. She started to swipe at them when he took her hand in his.

"You don't have to be ashamed of hurting. Pain is the price for loving."

"Thank you."

"For what?"

"For not telling me that the pain will go away. When…it…happened, that's what everyone said. 'Don't worry. The pain will go away in time.' But it hasn't. I don't think it ever will."

"The pain doesn't go away because your love hasn't gone away. You wouldn't want that, would you?"

"No," she said slowly. "I wouldn't."

Nicco hoped he hadn't blundered. Pretty talk wasn't his style, but he'd spoken from the heart and maybe he hadn't done too badly.

It was obvious that Scout was still raw from her parents' murders. Grief didn't have a timetable. Look at him. He was still grieving over Ruth's death, and that had been nearly three years ago.

Her voice was soft with the South lilting through it. Too soft to be talking about murder. Especially the murder of her parents, a murder that took place a scant year ago.

He was curious about Scout. For professional reasons only, he tried to convince himself. But he knew deep inside that the curiosity wasn't just professional, and he found that he wanted to know her better. There were shadows in her eyes, hinting that she'd learned some things the hard way. Was it the obvious—the murder of her parents— or something more?

"Is there someone special in your life?"

She shook her head. "Not since my fiancé dumped me."

"What happened?"

"Bradley Middleton showed up in my life

shortly after my parents were killed, just when I needed a prince charming."

"And?"

"He took me out, treated me like a princess. Within a couple of weeks, he asked me to marry him. I said yes. I can't believe how stupid I was. I started planning a wedding and Bradley left for New York."

"Just like that?"

"Yeah. Just like that."

"Has there been anyone since?"

"No. I'd rather stay home with a good book than be set up on a blind date. Or go to a singles' event."

"You and me both."

"It's better to be alone than to be with someone who isn't right. My mother always told me not to settle. To hold out for my 'one and only.'"

"Your fiancé was a jerk. He didn't deserve you."

"That's what I told myself." A mischievous smile turned up her lips. "Bradley's the kind of man who lights up a room by leaving it."

Nicco laughed deeply.

She directed a laser-sharp gaze at him. "What about you?"

"I stick to work."

"Looks like we have that in common."

They sat back and regarded each other.

"You're not so bad, Santonni," she said at last.

"Same goes, McAdams."

The accord between them startled Nicco. The last thing he wanted was to fall for a reporter. With that self-administered reminder, he reined in the unwanted feelings Scout roused in him and did what he did best: the job.

Scout had a network of CIs, just as the police had theirs. Confidential informants were a reporter's bread and butter. The best CIs were clued in to what was hot on the street often before the cops were.

So when Bug called, saying he had information about Crane, she could hardly contain her excitement. Bug, aka Terrence Howard, had given her viable tips in the past. She'd asked him to keep his ear to the ground for any information about union bosses, especially Leonard Crane.

Not only was Bug plugged in to what went on in the shadier parts of the city, he was a veritable genius when it came to computers. Give him a lead and he'd ferret out any and everything there was to be found.

"When and where?" she asked.

He gave her a time and location.

"I'll be there."

She relayed the information to Nicco, who

frowned when he heard the location. "No way. That area's bad news."

"It's not the best," she agreed. "But I didn't have a choice."

"Of course you did. You could have said no."

"This is important. Bug may have stumbled across something big. He's come through for me before."

"Doesn't mean he can't be used to get to you." Frustration edged Nicco's words.

"I don't need a babysitter."

"Maybe you've forgotten about the shots and the falling beams."

"I haven't forgotten anything. Including watching my parents being murdered."

When she grabbed her purse, Nicco blocked her way. "I don't like it. I can meet your CI for you."

"He's not going to talk to you." Bug was skittish at best. He'd scurry away like a scared rabbit if he saw Nicco, big and tough and totally intimidating, arrive in her place.

"I smell a setup. If you weren't so intent on getting the goods on Crane, you'd see it, too. Think. Why is this guy calling you now? When was the last time you heard from him?"

"A couple of weeks ago."

"Don't you get it? He wants to get you alone. Make you vulnerable."

"You'll be with me." She was confident Nicco would keep her safe. He tried to stare a capitulation out of her—she recognized the tactic, having used it herself on reluctant interview subjects—but she wasn't giving in.

"Doesn't mean you don't have to act smart. You've let this obsession blind you. Listen to your gut," he said. "I learned that on the schoolyard. Nothing changed when I was deployed. Your gut feels things before your head can process them. What is your gut telling you right now?"

"It's telling me I have to do this." She slung her purse over her shoulder and threw back her shoulders, settling the matter. "I'm going. The question is, am I going alone?"

SIX

Even at 11:00 p.m., the streets weren't empty. Nor were they quiet. But the noises were of a different type than those of the day. Furtive. Sly. Several men and a few women loitered in the doorways of buildings long since abandoned.

Those brave enough to dare to visit this sector of the city knew the wisdom of keeping gazes averted, hands in their pockets. Occasionally a curious look was directed at Scout and Nicco, but it was quickly redirected, as though whoever dared to commit the act of meeting a stranger's gaze in this no-man's land understood the folly of the breach of protocol.

An overturned car, windows smashed and tires stripped, slumped in the middle of the street, graffiti scrawled across the door. A single streetlight cast a weak yellow glow, a stalwart holdout in an area where every other light had either burnt out or been knocked out.

Night pressed in on her from all sides, causing

Scout to tremble; she felt Nicco's arm drop reassuringly across her shoulders. Though she told herself she could have handled the meeting on her own, she pressed closer to him, grateful for his presence. He carried himself with a quiet grace. He wasn't quite as big as his brother, but he still topped six feet by a good three inches.

A quick movement at her side caused her to jump, heart in her throat. She swallowed thickly. "Bug."

Bug, named for his oversize glasses, gave a little giggle. "McAdams. You came." A frown dug its way between his brows as he took in Nicco's presence. "You was s'pposed to come alone."

"Get over it," Nicco said. "I'm here. And I'm not going anywhere."

Bug's gaze darted from Nicco to Scout and back again. "Okay. I guess."

Scout knew her part. "Did you bring what you said you would?"

Bug nodded. "Don't I always deliver?" He had contacts all over the city. As he was fond of saying, what he didn't know or couldn't find out wasn't worth knowing or finding.

She didn't pay for information—no reputable reporter did—but she compensated Bug in other ways. His sister was in the shelter where Scout volunteered. Because of Bug's lifestyle, he didn't feel he could visit her there. Scout made sure the girl had the little extras that meant so much, like her favorite shampoo, new jeans, an occasional pair of the latest sneakers.

"Uh, Ms. McAdams, I 'ppreciate what you've done for Janeen." Though Bug had thanked her over the course of their relationship, there was an urgency to his words that was new.

"I'm happy to help her." The truth was, Scout would have helped the girl regardless of her arrangement with Bug, but she knew it was important to him that he give something in return.

"I know. Still…thanks."

Tension in Bug's voice alerted her that something was off, but she couldn't identify what it was. Fear whispered through her.

Even in the dim light, she could make out the sweat on his palms, the jittery dance of his feet on the wet pavement. Why was he so nervous?

Scout looked at the drive in her hand. If Bug had come through, she'd be that much closer to proving that Crane was involved in the murders of four union bosses and that of her parents.

Nicco nudged her elbow. "Time to go." Urgency scraped his voice, as though he, too, had picked up on Bug's nerves.

"Okay." She turned to say goodbye to Bug, but he'd already melted into the night.

Nicco nudged her forward. "C'mon. Something doesn't feel right." As though conjured up by his words, two shadows loomed before them. "Stay behind me," he said in a low voice. "What's up, guys?"

"We just want a word with the lady here," the larger of the men said, wielding a broken beer bottle. "We got no beef with you, so you can get lost. No harm, no foul."

Nicco broadened his stance. "Not gonna happen."

"Too bad. Hate to mess up that pretty face of yours." The last was said with a sneer.

Scout squinted to make out the men's faces. "Who are you?"

"Us? You could say that we're messengers. Someone wants you to mind your own business. You poked your nose where it don't belong one too many times."

The two men separated, the smaller one advancing toward Scout while Nicco took on the larger of the two. She knew her way around a fight. After her parents' deaths, she'd made sure she could take care of herself. She didn't wait for the attack but shot out her arm. The base of her palm torqued off a rigid arm for maximum power, and she drilled her hand into his nose.

Blood spurted and poured down his face, and he automatically put his hands up to staunch the flow. She pressed her advantage and gave a high kick to his thigh.

The hatred in his eyes promised retribution. When he moved in, she went to a crouch. "You think you're gonna take me down, little girl?"

"I aim to try."

His superior strength was in his favor, but she wasn't without moves of her own.

When he drew back to punch her, she trapped his hand, rotated against the joint, then rolled over, bringing him with her to the ground.

The breath knocked out of him, he didn't immediately get up. She took advantage of that and flipped to her feet. While her moves were first-rate, courtesy of her sensei, her opponent had the advantage of a longer reach and greater strength.

By this time, he had gotten to his feet as well. She kept a distance between her and the man who looked at her like she was prey to his hunter. The gleam in his eyes and curl of his lips told her that was exactly how he thought of her and that he was enjoying the fight.

Every fight scene she'd witnessed in action movies came back to her, and she fought the urge to taunt him with something ridiculous like "You want a piece of me? Bring it on."

Though she was a small enough target as it was, she angled her body so that her silhouette provided even less mass and shifted her weight forward on the balls of her feet to give her next move greater momentum, then delivered an elbow directly to his gut, sending him to his knees. A final kick to his chest sent him sprawling to the ground once more. The surprise on his face would have been comical if she'd been in the mood to laugh. As it was, she was scrabbling for any advantage.

He let out a hoarse *whuff,* but he still had some fight in him. Rage flaring in his eyes, he snagged her ankle, yanked her to the ground alongside him. She did a face-plant on the filthy street. Her vision grayed, and she struggled against unconsciousness. She fought against it and, seeing the man's gun holstered at his side, grabbed it and held it on him as she got to her feet.

"You fight like a little girl," she said.

The glare the assailant sent her way was full of hatred, but she didn't flinch under it. Instead, she lifted her chin and stared him down, all the while keeping the weapon trained on him.

In the meantime, Nicco was dealing with the other man. Nicco rammed his fist into his opponent's jaw. The man staggered, lurched to the side but didn't go down. Nicco moved to his left, hunkered over, then grabbed his man's leg and ripped it off the ground. While the man floundered, Nicco propelled him sideways so that he toppled onto his buddy.

At any other time, Scout would have admired

his skill, but the thug wasn't out. She saw him reach for his phone, tap a couple of keys.

Nicco must have also seen the action and come to the same conclusion she had. "They're not alone," he shouted. "Run."

Nicco grabbed Scout's hand, inadvertently causing her to drop the gun. They didn't dare stop for it, and he pulled her along with him. Her shorter legs couldn't match his stride.

"Go," she said when the heavy footsteps behind them grew closer. "It's me they want."

He ignored that and picked her up—she weighed less than the tactical pack he'd routinely carried as a Ranger—and ran as though their lives depended on it. Which they did.

His gaze landed on a faint depression in the wall of a warehouse. He pushed Scout inside, flattened her to the cinder-block wall, then pressed against her back, sheltering her body with his.

Smells, dank and putrid, rose from the ancient wood.

She trembled, the fine bones of her body so fragile he feared he'd crush her. "Nicco—"

"Shh."

Boots pounded close, too close. Nicco tensed. If the men spotted Scout and him… He didn't allow his thoughts to go any further. He could take two men, possibly three, but he'd counted four sets of footsteps.

In the Rangers, he'd fought off four tangos more than once, but he had Scout to think of. Her safety came first. If he went down, she'd be at the mercy of the men. Despite his order to the contrary, she'd stayed and fought at his side. Though she was only a little bit of a thing, she had some pretty fancy moves.

The fading slap of feet told him that their pursuers had run past them. He waited. Listened. "I think we've lost them."

Her breath came in little pants.

He cupped her shoulders, turned her to face him. "Hey, it's all right." He pressed her head to his chest and held her, just held her, until her shaking subsided.

She lifted her head, her gaze warm on his. "How long did you think you could run carrying me?"

"As long as it took."

"You Rangers are a breed apart."

A breed apart. Scout had spoken only the truth. Nicco had risked his life for her with no thought of himself. How did you thank someone for such a sacrifice? Words were inadequate, but still she tried. "Thank you."

The reassuring words she'd expected didn't

come. Instead it was a harsh order. "Don't ever tell me to leave you again. And the next time I tell you to move, you move," he all but growled as they walked back to where he'd parked his truck. But she knew it wasn't anger that prompted the words.

"I wasn't about to leave you there alone."

"You're the target. I can take care of myself."

"Oh," she said, light scorn working its way into her tone. "When did you become bullet-proof? Those men chasing us had guns, in case you didn't notice."

Nicco scowled. "You're going to be hurting by the time you get home."

"Too late. I already am." The step she took was wobbly, but she kept walking until he took her arm and pulled her to him.

"You all right?" he asked, and she knew he was inquiring about more than aches and pains.

"Yeah." After he helped her into the truck, she huddled in the corner of the passenger side. "I'm sorry."

"Yeah, well, you should be." The gruffness of his tone was tempered by gentle concern. "Did you think I'd have left you to face those thugs yourself?"

"I wasn't thinking." That was honest. She hadn't been thinking at all, her only thoughts on surviving.

"No. Just like you weren't thinking when you insisted on going to meet your CI in a part of town that anyone with brains goes out of their way to avoid."

Enough was enough. She'd apologized. What more did he want? "You were right, okay?" Anger splashed through the words.

"I'm trying to keep you alive." His voice had lost its hard edge.

"He set me up."

Scout couldn't keep the hurt from her voice. Though she and Bug weren't friends, she'd thought they had a working relationship of mutual respect. She'd been wrong.

"Someone got to him," Nicco agreed. "Used him."

Tim Anderson, the relief agent, met them at the house. After checking out the house, Nicco motioned her inside, then talked in a low voice to the other agent before joining her in the kitchen where she was making tea.

"You'll be safe for the night. As long as you stay inside."

She heard the warning in his voice. "I'm not going anywhere."

The impatience in his eyes softened, and when he spoke again, it was with warm concern. "You sure you're all right?"

She summoned a smile. "Go. I'll be fine."

His gaze moved over her, and she knew she hadn't fooled him.

"I'll be fine," she repeated.

"So you said. Why don't I believe it?" His chin dipped to her hands, now balled into fists at her side.

Flushing under his astute gaze, she opened the hands she hadn't known she'd clenched and loosened her fingers one by one. She gave him a gentle shove toward the door. "I'm a big girl. I can take care of myself."

After Nicco left, she plugged in the thumb drive, unsurprised when she discovered it blank. Bug hadn't expected her to live long enough to look at it.

Her nightly prayers took longer than usual as she asked for the strength to forgive.

Exhausted as she was, sleep didn't come easily, and when it did, it was restless and disturbed.

The nightmare returned, brutal in its clarity. It yanked her from sleep and beat her up mercilessly. Her tormentors chased her through a rain-darkened night, laughing gleefully at her fear. She wouldn't let them win. Wouldn't let them break her.

When she woke, it was with the sheet tangled in her legs, her breathing short and choppy. A vicious headache beat at her temples.

Good. That meant she'd fought the men who

had killed her parents. She hadn't given in. She looked up, saw that daylight lined the edges of the window shades and was grateful that it was almost time to get up.

She was no wimp. She'd trained at a dojo and could take down men twice her size. Though, no matter how strong she was, no matter how much she trained, she couldn't kick the nightmares. She did visualizations, and, most of the time, she controlled the fear. If it caught her off guard, though, like last night, the fear controlled her.

Her struggle with the imaginary assailants had left her exhausted, with painful memories of when she'd been helpless to do anything to save her parents hot and fresh in her mind.

Harshly awake now, she dropped her head into her hands, trying to shake off the pain, the fear, the helplessness. Weary of trying to deny the memories entrance, she let them in. They had been celebrating that night, she and her parents, upon the publication of her first story in the city section of the paper.

On the way home from the restaurant, a detour had taken them through an unfamiliar area where two men had carjacked them. The gunmen had killed her parents in front of her, then put a bullet in her lower shoulder, believing her to be dead just as her parents were. Somehow, she'd lived through it.

And then wished she hadn't.

People told her she was fortunate to be alive. A bullet in the shoulder didn't feel fortunate. Nor did the nightmares that had plagued her ever since. All of that on top of losing the two most important people in the world to her made her feel distinctly unfortunate. She hadn't even been able to attend her parents' funeral because she'd been in the hospital recovering at the time.

After saying a prayer, she took a few minutes to go through the relaxation exercises a therapist had suggested. *Breathe.* The familiar directive steadied her, and she felt her heartbeat gradually slow to a more normal pace even as her soul cried out to her parents in protest.

Why did you have to be taken so soon? Why did we have to take that route home? Why? I wasn't ready to lose you. Either of you.

Granted, she was an adult, but there was never a good time to lose parents, never a good time to become an orphan, never a good time to say goodbye.

Memories of her mother flowed through her mind. An English professor and a writer, Georgette had loved books with a passion surpassed only by the love she had for her family.

Wearily, Scout pushed herself out of bed and made it to the shower. Hot water and soap, prayer and work, were her recipe for getting through the day after a long night. Now that the adrenaline had worn off, she was feeling the effects of last night's fight. For the second time in only three days, she ached all over. Her own fault. She could have run as Nicco had ordered.

But that wasn't who she was. No, she silently amended. It wasn't who she *wanted* to be.

As was her routine, she flipped on the television to a twenty-four-hour news channel. She brewed coffee and poured three cups, knowing Nicco would arrive shortly to change places with the other operative. She offered a cup to Anderson, who accepted it with a grateful smile.

When Nicco arrived, she gestured to the coffee.

He frowned when he looked at her, then helped himself to a cup. "Bad night?"

"You could say that."

"Nightmare." It was a statement, not a question. She nodded, wanting to leave it there, but he pumped her for details. "Have them often?"

"No. Maybe. A couple this week. Last night... it brought things back."

"Tell me."

The simple command caused her to stop and consider. Outside of her counselor, she'd never shared the nightmares with anyone, not even Olivia. Why was she even considering talking to Nicco about them?

"Sometimes I'm running, like last night. Other times, I'm fighting. Trying to save my parents. Except I can't." Her voice thickened, and she coughed to clear it. "Everything seems bigger than life. The men who...who shot my parents are giants."

Nicco took her hands in his.

"They loom over me, laughing. I try to take the guns from them, but they throw me against a wall." A laugh came harshly. "Of course, none of that is true. The men aren't really giants. And they didn't throw me against a wall. They shot me, left me for dead in the car." Her breathing grew fast and shallow as she found herself back at that night.

His grip on her hands tightened. "It's all right. You're here. With me."

Breathe. "Here. With you." She held on to the words as she would a lifeline. "Thank you."

"For what?"

"For being here. For listening." Needing a distraction, she pointed to the empty drive, intending to tell him about it, but he hitched his chin at the TV.

"Look."

A picture of Bug filled the television screen.

"Terrence Howard, a known informant, was found dead in the southeast section of the city last night. More to follow."

She flipped through the other news channels, looking for more information on the story. Details were scarce. Either the police didn't know much, or they weren't sharing. Probably both.

This was no coincidence. She knew it, and from the hard set of Nicco's mouth, so did he.

"They didn't want to leave any loose ends," he said.

"Who is 'they'?" she asked, though she knew. *They* were the people who wanted her dead.

"That's what we're going to find out."

Knowing someone hated her enough to kill her was surreal. A bolt of fear ripped through her chest. She fought it, but the intensity of it mocked her efforts. How long could she keep pretending that she wasn't afraid? She was Scout McAdams. Intrepid journalist. Fearless seeker of truth.

She was a fraud.

When people found out that she wanted to run and hide, they'd despise her. Almost as much as she despised herself.

SEVEN

Nicco didn't like the shadows under her eyes any more than he did the bruise that blossomed on her cheek, a mute reminder of last night. If she'd stayed behind him as he'd ordered… He shook his head at the futility of the speculation. That wasn't who Scout McAdams was.

Her courage notwithstanding, she had an innocence that some might mistake for naivete. He knew she was anything but naive. Having witnessed the murder of her parents, she had had a crash course in the dark side of life. Still, she managed to look at the world with optimism and a determination to make it better.

After some discussion, he and Scout agreed to tell her coworkers that she'd been receiving threatening letters and that he was there to keep an eye on her. It was best to stick as close to the truth as possible in such situations.

He drove her to the paper, found a corner from which he could both watch her and set up his laptop and did a FaceTime consult with Shelley, who was now back in Atlanta. Using the shorthand of S&J operatives, he filled her in on what had happened. As she was friends with both Olivia and Scout, Shelley had a personal interest in the case.

"You've been busy," his boss said after listening to his account of the three attempts on Scout's life.

"Someone really wants our girl out of the way." He frowned at his use of the phrase *our girl* and was relieved when Shelley didn't comment on it, though she did raise a brow.

"Sounds like it. Knowing Scout, I don't expect her to bow out of the investigation gracefully and leave it to us."

He tapped his fingers on the battered desk where he'd set up shop. "Right the first time."

"Do you think she's right and this goes back to her parents' murders? And what about the union? Is it connected, like she believes?"

"Someone thinks she's close to finding the truth. How the union and Crane fit into it, I don't know. Yet."

"But you'll find out."

"You can count on it."

Nicco spent the first part of the morning digging up stories on the union murders and learning as much as he could. They were grisly affairs with the victims' necks slashed. Rumors of graft and corruption shrouded Savannah's unions. No wonder Georgette McAdams had decided to base a book on them.

Next, he looked at the newspaper's coverage of Scout's parents' murders. Since her mother was a celebrity, the stories were extensive, but after the first few days, they had rehashed the background about Georgette and Ron McAdams. Nicco knew what that meant: the police had run out of leads and there was no new information.

If a murder wasn't solved in the first forty-eight hours, it was likely to go unsolved. Though the McAdamses' case was still officially open, Nicco understood that it had been put on the back burner. Unless something broke, it would remain there. No wonder Scout was so determined to find the truth.

Scout slipped on a sundress splashed with giant poppies. She was meeting Olivia Santonni for dinner. The two friends made it a point to have dinner together at least once a month. Since Olivia, a busy lawyer, had married, her free time was limited, but she always made time for their dinner.

Scout was especially grateful they could get together tonight. Over the last week, she and Nicco had settled into a kind of routine. His presence was both comforting and unsettling, and she needed a dose of Olivia's special brand of friendship to ground her.

In between covering the Duchess's events, Scout continued her investigation into her parents' murders, but even she had to admit that it was stalled. All she had were her mother's suspicions about Crane, hardly enough to take to the police.

No new letters had arrived, nor had any more attempts been made on her life. She wanted to believe that the threat was over, had said as much to Nicco, but he wasn't convinced. He'd voiced his displeasure at tonight's outing, but she pointed out that Anderson would be nearby and that she'd be fine. In addition, Nicco needed sleep. No one, not even a Ranger, could go indefinitely without sleep.

The restaurant was a new one, specializing in Bolivian food. Always eager to try something unfamiliar, Scout looked forward to ordering an exotic dish.

After cheek-bussing, she and Olivia slid into a booth. Scout sent her friend an admiring look. "You're glowing. Marriage agrees with you."

Olivia dipped her head. "Love agrees with me." A soft blush spread across her cheeks.

"It shows. Something's different." Scout studied her friend, trying to identify what it was. "You're pregnant."

The blush deepened. "I just learned yesterday. How did you guess?"

"That glow. It says everything. What did Sal say when you told him?"

"He's over the moon. He's already planning on adding a nursery to the house and is making noises about buying a miniature football."

Scout grinned at the thought of Olivia's husband, big and tough, and at the same time incredibly gentle. "He's going to make a great father. And you'll be a wonderful mother."

"What about you? Is there a new man in your life?"

To Scout's chagrin, a picture of Nicco flashed through her mind. "No," she said at last.

"Really?" Olivia raised a skeptical brow. "That 'no' sounded pretty weak. As in, you have met someone and you don't want to tell me." She eyed Scout shrewdly. "You haven't said anything about Nicco. I expected you to tear into me about hiring him behind your back. Now I'm wondering why you haven't."

"I was getting to it."

"Were you? Or were you slow in bringing him up because you like him?"

"What's not to like?" Scout countered with a lightness she was far from feeling.

"Nothing that I can see. The Santonni men are pretty irresistible." Olivia laughed merrily. "I ought to know."

"You shouldn't have hired him without talking with me first," Scout said, turning the conversation serious.

Red crept in to Olivia's fair complexion. "I know. I was wrong, but I was worried about you."

"Thank you for that," Scout said gently. "But it should have been my decision."

"I'm sorry."

Scout reached for her friend's hand. "I know you're worried, and Nicco's not so bad."

Olivia sat back, regarding Scout with knowing eyes. "You like him, don't you?"

"Maybe," she managed to say.

A satisfied gleam lit Olivia's eyes and then vanished as her expression sobered. "Now to the hard stuff. What's going on that someone wants to kill you for?"

Scout told her friend about her mother's suspicions about Crane.

"Are you investigating anything else?" Olivia asked. "Anyone else?"

"I'm writing a series of stories about Patrice Newtown's charity, Homes for Everyone."

"Sounds harmless enough."

"Except for having to choke down chicken din-

ners and make nice with a bunch of society ladies, it's okay."

"So it's got to be your mother's story. Is it
worth your life?"

When Scout came down the stairs the following morning, Nicco did a double take. She wore
a yellow dress and had done something smoky to
her eyes that made her look both intensely feminine and a little mysterious.

"What's with the getup?" he asked.

"Another one of the Duchess's events." Scout
wrinkled her nose. "A fashion show."

"You look like one of the models."

"You're kidding, right? No way could I com-
pete with those models. Even if I wanted to wear
ridiculous clothes and starve myself until I looked
like a stick, I'm about a foot too short."

To his eyes, she was beautiful, even though the
shadows under her eyes made her look vulnerable. He found it impossible to turn away from the
troubled look he saw there. Unaccountably annoyed, he started to say something, then stopped
himself.

There was more to this woman than he knew,
and he doubted she allowed many to see beyond
the mask of the tough, no-nonsense reporter she
wore so easily and with such assurance. He found

himself curious to discover who the real Scout McAdams was.

She was smart, funny and fearless. A potent combination. And an appealing one. So why was he fighting admitting that he might actually like her?

Maybe it was a good thing. He didn't need a relationship. He had a career to concentrate on. No woman, even one as engaging as Scout McAdams, was going to derail that. It shamed him to admit it, but he was afraid, afraid to feel something for another woman after losing Ruth. Fear didn't sit easily on his shoulders, but honesty forced him to acknowledge it.

When his phone buzzed a few minutes later, he frowned on seeing that it was his boss. Shelley wouldn't be calling when she knew he was on duty unless it was important.

"Can't, boss," Nicco said when Shelley told him that he was needed to testify at a court case in which S&J had been instrumental in bringing down a corrupt judge. "I'm with Scout today."

"Get your relief to take over." A harried sigh sounded over the phone. "I'm sorry about the last-minute notice, but the other two operatives are UC. Their assignments were due to end last night, but things took a turn south. I just got the call."

Nicco heard the worry in her voice. He under-

stood about undercover work. Rarely did everything go as planned.

"Anderson was on duty last night. He's due
back tonight."

"Can't be helped. Besides, you won't be in
court more than an hour or two. You can get
back to Scout when you're done and Anderson
can catch up on his beauty sleep." A long pause.
"Is there something going on that I should know
about? Something other than the assignment, that
is?"

"No." His answer was short to the point of
being rude. "Just doing my job," he said in an
attempt to soft-pedal the brusqueness of his response.

Nicco accepted that he wasn't going to get out
of testifying. Normally he didn't mind court duty,
but he didn't like being away from Scout any
more than he had to be. The other night's incident
was a reminder that her enemies hadn't let up.

He relayed the change of plans to Scout and
Anderson.

"No problem," Anderson said with a barely
concealed wince. "I can take Ms. McAdams
wherever she needs to go."

"Including a fashion show?" Scout teased.

Anderson swallowed. "Like I said, wherever
you need to go."

Nicco didn't blame him for his reluctance. Attending a ladies' luncheon and fashion show bordered on cruel and unusual punishment.

Ordinarily, he'd have asked Sal, but his brother was attending a doctor's appointment with Olivia. No way would Nicco drag him away from that.

"It's settled," Scout said to Nicco. "You go testify and put bad guys away and Anderson and I'll go scope out the latest fashions."

Nicco expected Anderson to make a joke, but the man looked slightly green. "Buck up, man."

Scout reached up to skim her lips over Nicco's jaw. "Don't worry. What's going to happen to me at a fashion show?"

EIGHT

Scout had cause to remember her words when, ten minutes before she was supposed to leave for the show, Anderson collapsed, clutching his left side and groaning. A call to 911 brought emergency personnel to her town house, who, after a brief exam, announced that the operative was having an appendicitis attack.

Still, Anderson tried to get up from the stretcher where the EMTs had him strapped down.

"No way," she told him. "You go to the hospital. I'll be fine." She'd have chucked the whole thing and accompanied him, but her boss, Gerald Daniels, had been uncharacteristically adamant that she cover the show.

"Nicco will have my head," Anderson muttered.

"Leave Nicco to me."

She made it to the event on time and then wished she hadn't. The luncheon was typical society fare, though the chicken had been replaced by some other meat equally rubbery. Scout did her best not to think about what she was eating and entertained herself by watching the other guests and making up stories about them.

The blue-haired lady with the matching dress, definitely one of the "marching matrons," as Scout had labeled the women who had an abundance of money, class and time and devoted themselves to good works, was in reality employed by the FBI. The woman dressed all in pink, right down to the bows on her pink pumps, secretly moonlighted as a dancer in an all-night club where she worked for tips.

And the lady with the purple turban that clashed violently with her orange suit had to be a spy for a rival fashion house to the one featured at today's event.

Scout looked down at her own attire. Her mouth turned up in a brief smile as she wondered if any of those individuals present might mistake her for one of the city's elite. The forsythia-yellow sheath dress and matching jacket paired with stiletto heels in coral wasn't her usual style. Her typical workday uniform of jeans, T-shirt and high-top sneakers wouldn't cut it for a luncheon sponsored by the Duchess.

She picked at a limp salad, all the while wishing it were a double deluxe cheeseburger with a side of fries and washed down with a chocolate malt. After risking one bite of the pinkish-brown blob on the dinner plate that she supposed was some kind of meat, she decided she'd do better to stick with the salad.

Patrice Newtown made her way toward Scout. The four-inch heels she sported didn't slow her pace in the least. In fact, they seemed to propel her forward. Scout estimated the woman's shoes alone to be around twelve hundred dollars. She admired the shoes, even while accepting that she wasn't likely to ever have the kind of money that allowed for such luxuries.

The woman didn't walk, she glided, as if the money that was associated with the Newtown family paved her every step.

"Scout McAdams. Just the person I wanted to see." Lips pulled in a slight pout, the lady looked about. "You're definitely the most interesting person here."

Scout lifted a brow.

Patrice nodded emphatically. "You're exactly the kind of woman this city needs. Intelligent. Vibrant. Passionate. And your roots run deep."

The Duchess frowned when she saw there wasn't an empty chair at Scout's table. A waiter hurried to put a chair in place. She crossed one elegantly shaped leg over the other and sat back. Her expression was one of speculation. "I want you on my team. More than writing articles about my charity."

"As an extra woman?" Scout asked with a wry twist of her lips. A single man or woman who didn't chew with his or her mouth open and could speak with reasonable intelligence was a sought-after commodity on the guest list of many hostesses.

"As an essential woman. You would be an asset in any gathering. With your contacts and panache, you're just the kind of individual we want serving on our board."

Scout shook her head. "I'm flattered, but I'm not society board material. I'm more the sell-raffle-tickets-in-the-church-basement type."

"Don't sell yourself short. It's beneath you."

"You've been frank with me, so I'll do the same. I don't like society affairs. I normally avoid them like the plague. Same with the people who run them." She paused, gauging how that sat with Newtown. "For the most part, the affairs are stuffy and boring and the money spent in putting them on would be better spent on the charities they're supposed to benefit."

"Don't stop now," the lady said, her eyes full of amusement. "Give it to me with both barrels."

"Okay. How much did today's shindig cost?"

"Ten thousand dollars."

"Why not just donate that amount to your charity to begin with and save all the fuss and bother of putting on a show?"

Scout already knew the answer, but she wanted to hear Newtown explain it in her own words. Getting to know a subject—which was how Scout regarded the Duchess—meant speaking her language. Scout knew she was woefully ignorant in society-speak.

Newtown held up a finger. "First, we'll make five times that amount in ticket sales and donations. Second, this event attracts influential women."

She directed a discreet finger at a woman dressed head-to-toe in lavender, including the animal carrier at her feet. "That's Julia Kramer. The mayor's wife. She'll go home and decide she needs to throw an event of her own, one to top mine." Newtown waved a hand, a dismissive gesture to what was obviously an old rivalry. "That doesn't matter. Julia is a publicity hound and will do anything to get her name in the papers. What matters is that her shindig, as you call these things, will bring in fifty thousand dollars or more. She'll present her husband, the mayor, with a check for the new shelter. Do you see the lady toward the front, the one with the two security men hovering around her? That's the governor's wife. She'll do the same."

Scout looked about for Christine Daniels, the

wife of the paper's publisher, expecting her to be present, but didn't see her. Probably the lady had decided to send a check and forego the fashion show. Scout would have done the same if she'd been able. "So these events are contagious. Like a virus."

Newtown laughed again. "I knew I picked the right person to cover these things."

Scout had wondered how the Duchess had managed to pull off requesting a specific reporter to cover her events before remembering that the paper's publisher and Newtown were both supporters of the opera. Such bonds were common among the ultra-wealthy.

"You'll bring your trademark no-nonsense tone to the articles you write," Newtown continued. "That will attract interest from people who normally avoid social affairs 'like the plague.'"

Chastened, Scout blushed. "I'm sorry. I didn't mean—"

"Of course you did. I want that. I want you to be as blunt and honest as you are right now, writing the kind of articles that will make ordinary people consider contributing to the cause. Even if it's only five dollars."

With a flash of shame, Scout realized she'd come today with her mind already made up about Newtown and her charity. "I'm sorry," she repeated, this time meaning it. "I'll do my best."

"That's all I ask." Newtown sat back. "The foundation means everything to me. My late husband…" Newtown's voice caught. "It was his dream to do something to help the city's homeless. Before he died, I promised I'd carry on what he started."

Sunlight, streaming through the Palladian styled windows, caught the delicate tears on her cheeks, turning them into glistening drops. The woman even cried in a graceful manner. Her eyes didn't go puffy; her nose didn't turn red. There were no noisy sobs, only the quiet trail of tears down her perfectly sculpted cheekbones.

Scout wanted to dislike her, if only because the Duchess had caused her to be taken from real journalism, but there was nothing in the woman with which to find fault. Her concern for the homeless seemed sincere. She was a society lady, through and through.

Unlike herself, Scout thought. Her idea of a perfect Saturday afternoon was taking in a game and eating a loaded hot dog at the ballpark.

She felt like a fraud, sitting here in her dress and heels. She picked at the unidentifiable meat on her plate, more to have something to do with her hands than because she was hungry.

"Awful, isn't it?"

Scout barely contained her surprise. "Uh…it's not bad."

"Be honest. It's dreadful. But it's the best we can do if we want to keep costs down and make more money for the shelter." The polish of finishing school and summers in Europe wafted through her voice.

"Good point."

Patrice Newtown smiled, drawing Scout's attention to the razor-edged cheekbones in the beautiful face. Her smile, like the rest of her, was dazzling, a combination of feminine warmth and charm. "I may have been born with a silver spoon in my mouth, but I know how to be practical. Especially when it involves something close to my heart, like…" Her eyes filled with tears, tears she didn't bother to wipe away. "Excuse me, it's just that this is so very important."

Disarmed by the woman's frank emotion, Scout reached out and touched the lady's hand. She couldn't help noticing the titanium Breguet with the carbon-fiber face, and though she didn't know much about high-end timepieces and cared even less, she recognized that such a watch cost upward of ten thousand dollars.

She filed that away and yanked her attention back to what they'd been talking about. "It's all right. I'm the same way. My friend says that when my heart is engaged, my emotions leak out of my eyes."

The Duchess gave a delicate shake and then

smiled. "Thank you for saying that. The friend? Would that be Olivia Hammond Santonni? I've heard that you two are close."

Scout wasn't often taken by surprise, but the Duchess had managed to do just that. "How did you know?" While her stories were written for the public, she kept her private life just that: private.

"When I want someone on my team, I make it my business to know everything about her. So I did some digging on you. I liked what I found." Newtown eyed Scout shrewdly. "You're smart and savvy and have more than your share of moxie. You know as well as I do that for a woman to succeed she has to work twice as hard as a man to be considered half as good." Her forehead temporarily wrinkled before smoothing out once more.

Scout dipped her head in acknowledgement, reluctantly fascinated by this woman whom she'd first dismissed as all fluff and no substance. There was intelligence there, along with steely determination that said the Duchess would do whatever was necessary to achieve her goals.

"It's not fair, but it is what it is," the Duchess continued in a matter-of-fact voice. "That's why when I go after something, I don't accept no for an answer. I fight for what I want. I see the same in you."

No, Newtown wasn't the empty-headed social-ite Scout had first thought. There was grit beneath the rose-pink Chanel suit and Jimmy Choo footwear.

For as long as she could remember, she'd been able to size up people with only a glance, maybe a handshake. She was rarely wrong. Honesty forced her to admit that she may have misjudged Patrice Newtown. "You're different from what I thought."

If she'd expected the woman to take offense at the blunt statement, she was wrong.

"I'll take that as a compliment. You must be all kinds of put out with me, calling in favors and asking for you to cover my events. But you're the best and I wanted the best. Now's your opportunity to prove it." Newtown added the last with a bright spark of challenge.

"I'm not a society reporter," Scout pointed out, flattered but determined to speak her mind all the same. "I can't write the kind of pieces you're expecting."

"I don't expect anything but the truth. Be yourself. Write from an outsider's viewpoint. That will be far more powerful than the usual fluff pieces we get on these events." The Duchess wrinkled her nose. "Such pieces are necessary, but they won't attract the kind of attention I want for this project. People will see your byline and know that you won't sugarcoat anything. They'll expect the truth, and you'll give it to them."

Scout poked at what passed for meat on her plate and pulled a comical face. "Is it all right if I compare the food to that of a middle-school cafeteria?"

Patrice laughed, the tinkling sound one of unabashed delight. "I'd be disappointed if you didn't."

"Duchess?" A man appeared at her side, his manner differential. "We'll be ready to begin in three minutes."

"Thank you, Roderick." Newtown smiled at Scout's raised brow. "You probably think the name is ridiculous. Someone bestowed it upon me years ago and it stuck. It's meaningless, of course."

But Scout could tell the name pleased her.

Music signaled the start of the event.

The Duchess sat back. "Some of the designs are to-die-for. I already have my eye on several. Let's enjoy the show."

Scout had a feeling she'd just been treated to one.

Sal, who was S&J's operation chief in Savannah, intercepted Nicco at the courthouse. "Olivia's doctor's appointment ended early, so I headed over here. Don't come unglued, but Scout went to the fashion show on her own."

As Sal filled in the details on Anderson, Nicco slammed his fist into his palm. "Anderson should have ordered her to stay home."

"Cool it," Sal said, his voice calm in comparison to the storm that was brewing inside Nicco. "She's going to a society luncheon. The biggest danger there is choking on a piece of watercress."

"The last time she was at a society event, she was shot at," Nicco said.

Sal looked abashed. "You're right. But the lady has a mind of her own. No one orders her to do anything."

Nicco shot his older brother a dirty look while silently acknowledging that he was right about Scout. She wouldn't accept anyone telling her what she could and couldn't do. "Someone's already tried to take her out more than once. I don't want her out of my sight until we find whoever's behind this."

Sal raised a brow. "It's like that, is it?"

"No. Yeah." Nicco considered telling his brother to mind his own business but knew he wouldn't get away with it. "Maybe. How am I supposed to know?" Fear and frustration turned his words into a growl. He took a breath. "Is that how it was with you and Olivia?"

"Pretty much. There were some rough times, but we made it." Sal's eyes darkened. Nicco figured his brother was remembering the terror he'd experienced when Olivia had been kidnapped by someone she'd thought of as a friend. "If I'd have lost her..." He shook his head, obviously unwilling to go there. "She's everything to me. I want that for you, little brother."

Nicco swallowed his surprise. Sal wasn't given to voicing his feelings any more than Nicco was. For Sal to do so now was quietly moving. Embarrassed and touched, Nicco looked away.

Sal and Olivia had made something good for themselves. With their wedding less than a year behind them, they were totally in love. For the first time in his life, Nicco envied his brother.

Nicco thought of the contradictory feelings he had for Scout despite his best efforts to quell them. He admired her, respected her, liked her, even while telling himself that there could be nothing between them.

He knew she still grieved for her parents, for the lives that had been taken by violence, while he was still learning to deal with the aftermath of his last mission.

Any other time, Nicco would have been fascinated to hear his brother, the big bad Delta, talk about feelings, but at the moment all he cared about was knowing Scout was safe.

Scout left the luncheon with sore feet, a stomach that was grumbling its displeasure with the recent bland meal, and a revised opinion of the Duchess. The woman had a head on her shoulders, one that appeared good for more than simply providing a place for the two-carat diamond earrings she sported.

Scout was still annoyed at being derailed from her usual beat, but she was determined to give the story her best. Though she wasn't a fan of ladies' luncheons and fashion shows, she heartily approved of the cause.

Caught up in planning how she'd frame the story to highlight the plight of Savannah's homeless, she didn't give much attention to the rusted white pickup that was closing in fast. She tapped her brakes, the time-honored signal to tell the driver to back off. Rather than easing off, he closed the distance between the vehicles even more.

She shot the driver an annoyed look in the rearview mirror. Only a fool would try to pass on the road that narrowed as it approached a deep canyon. When she realized he intended to pass her despite the treacherous stretch, she edged to the side.

"Idiot," she muttered under her breath. "Go ahead, then, if you're in such an all-fired hurry, and get out of here."

She hugged the right shoulder of the road, but the truck refused to pass. Instead, it aimed right for her. Why hadn't she guessed his intention earlier?

Just when she thought the truck would ram her, the driver pulled sharply to the left and came alongside her, driving her into the rock face of the cliff. She started to scramble across the seat to the passenger side and found the door blocked by the embankment. She was trapped, but she wasn't going to make it easy.

No way would she be a victim. Never again. During the carjacking that had claimed her parents' lives, she'd cowered in the corner of the backseat. She hadn't fought, hadn't tried to save herself or, to her shame, her parents.

This time, she'd fight.

The driver yanked open the door and jerked her from the car, meaty hands gripping her shoulder. They smelled of cheap cologne and even cheaper beer. "Down on your knees." He pushed her to the gravel pavement.

More frightening than his words was his unmasked face. He didn't expect her to walk away from this. Just as the men who had murdered her parents hadn't expected anyone to walk away.

She'd worked with a sketch artist, but nothing had come of it.

The words of her sensei came back to her. *Use what you have.* She didn't have a weapon, but she had her brain. She sized up the man as a good ol' boy who didn't regard women as anywhere near equal to men. She'd use that against him.

"Please don't hurt me. Please." A sob punctuated the words as she worked to sound as pitiful as possible. She kept up the pleading, all the while working her foot from her shoe. It turned out the stilettos she'd complained about were going to come in handy after all.

"Quit your begging." He made a disgusted sound, then half turned away and pulled out his phone, murmuring a few words into it.

That was her opening. Shoe in hand, she sprang up and used the heel as she would a knife, plunging it deep into the side of his neck.

He yowled and spun to face her, dropping the knife as he clutched his neck with both hands. Blood spurted from the wound. She refused to feel guilty about inflicting the blow. She was fighting for her life.

No one's going to save you but yourself. Another piece of counsel from the sensei at the dojo where she practiced martial arts.

She scrambled for the knife and aimed it at the assailant's chest, her intention clear. If he came at her again, she'd use it and do so without hesitation. She didn't relish causing him more injury, but she wasn't about to let him kill her.

Eyes full of hate, he glared at her even as blood ran down his neck and onto his shoulder. "You'll pay for that." He jerked a handkerchief from his pocket and pressed it against the wound.

She gave him a moment to staunch the flow of blood before pulling out a roll of duct tape from a tool kit she kept in her trunk and binding his wrists and ankles together. Reruns of *MacGyver* had given her a deep appreciation for the wonders of the silver tape.

After securing his hands and feet, she ran to his truck and punctured a tire with his own knife. For good measure, she used it on the other three tires as well. It would be a tight squeeze, but she thought she could maneuver her car from where it was wedged against the canyon wall.

"Tell whoever hired you that I don't back down and I don't back off."

NINE

Nicco met Scout at the police station where she was giving a report. In spite of the fear and anger that fought for dominance inside of him, he couldn't help being impressed with the detail she included in her description of the man.

From a friend on the force, Nicco had heard that she'd not only saved herself but had subdued and bound the attacker as well. Unfortunately, the man had freed himself before the police had arrived. He must have walked away, seeing as how Scout had flattened his tires.

"Why didn't you call me?" He was barely keeping it together. Learning that Scout had been run off the road had nearly sent him over the edge. The unintentional metaphor would have caused him to smile on another occasion; now, he was too caught up in worry.

He should have been there, would have been there if he'd had his way.

"I was a little busy trying to stay alive. Then I

had to get my heart out of my throat and stuff it back in my chest," she retorted.

"Sorry." Nicco cupped her shoulders, studied her. "Are you all right?"

"Yes…" She drew out the word, as though unsure of its truthfulness. "No. But I will be."

He eyed the single stiletto that dangled from her hand. "Is that *the* shoe?"

She shook her head. "The mate. How did you hear about it?"

"Are you kidding? A hundred-pound woman fights off an attacker using nothing but a high heel? That's the stuff legends are made of." He was proud of her. At the same time, he wanted to wrap her in his arms, cart her off and keep her safe from anyone who would try to harm her.

His grip on her tightened as he thought of what could have happened, what would have happened, if she hadn't been so resourceful.

"Careful," she said.

"Sorry." He was mortified that his voice shook.

"I'm the one who was run off the road." She laid her fingertips on his arm. "I'm sorry if you were worried."

"You're one tough lady."

"That's reporter-lady to you. What're the chances they'll pick up this creep?"

"He's probably gone to ground. Hired help like

that have a dozen places to hide out until things cool down."

Though she kept up her usual brisk pace, her gaze stayed fixed to the sidewalk as though she was afraid to reveal how vulnerable she felt. Scout had more courage and guts than many men he'd met, but she was still a woman, vulnerable in ways that men weren't. A quick intake of breath had him turning sharply in her direction.

"Reaction setting in?" he guessed.

Another breath. Shakier this time. "Big time."

"You need to be home. Rest."

She squared her shoulders against the sugges-tion. Against him? "What I need is to write the piece on the fashion show while it's still fresh in my mind."

"You're thinking of the story? Now?" He couldn't mask his incredulity.

"I'm *thinking*," she stressed, "that I need to do my job."

"Sorry."

Her shoulders, stiff with resolve only a moment ago, drooped now. The defeated gesture had him wanting to wrap his arm around her, but he knew she wouldn't appreciate it.

He took her to the paper where she immedi-ately started writing the story. He'd have pre-ferred she work at home, but she pointed out that the office was closer and she wanted to get the story down as quickly as possible.

An hour. He'd give her an hour. No more. Then he was taking her home, whether she liked it or not. If she'd looked vulnerable earlier, she now looked fragile enough to break.

"How long?" he asked when the hour came and went.

She lifted her head long enough to throw him a challenging look. "As long as it takes." She tapped a key. A few seconds later, the printer spat out a sheet of paper. "There. What do you think?"

Nicco read the story, nodded. "It's good."

"You think so?"

But he'd run out of patience. "I *think* it's time you started using your head. Someone wants you to stop investigating. They want it enough to commit murder."

Scout kept to herself on the trip to her place. It was clear that Nicco was annoyed with her. She snuck a glance at the white-knuckled grip he had on the steering wheel. Scratch annoyed. Anger emanated from him in palpable waves, even as silence stretched between them, edgy and sharp and accusing.

When they reached her house, she let herself out of the truck without waiting for him and walked to the front door.

Nicco put his hand over hers when she went to unlock the door. "Stay here. I go in first, remember?"

Flustered that she'd forgotten the drill, she nodded. A few minutes later, he gave the all-clear signal. He waited until she'd poured herself a glass of water. Wanting a reprieve from the lecture she knew was coming, she sipped slowly.

He pulled a kitchen chair from the table, turned it around, straddled it. Pointed to the chair opposite. She sat. From the set of his mouth, the reprieve was over.

She decided to go on the offensive. "Why don't you say something? Anything?"

"You handled yourself today. But what's going to happen when you find yourself in a situation you can't handle?"

A dozen retorts came to her mind. She rejected all but one. "I can't stop living my life because of some threats."

"You're too smart to say something that stupid."

"Stupid? So now I'm stupid?"

Nicco slashed the air with an impatient gesture. "You know what I mean. You could have been killed today."

And then she understood. He'd been afraid. For her.

"I'm sorry."

Surprise, then wariness, crossed his face. "Sorry?"

"For scaring you."

"Nothing is worth your life. Nothing. Including this investigation."

She wanted to protest, but she didn't want to destroy the fragile peace that hovered between them. "I'll be more careful. I promise."

"I don't want you to just be careful. I want you to stay alive."

"There are some things worth risking your life for. You had to have felt that, being a Ranger."

"That's—"

"Different? Is that what you were going to say? Why? Because you're a man and I'm a woman?" With her thumb and index finger, she rubbed the space between her brows.

"No. Because that was my job."

"This is more than my job."

"How do you mean?"

"It's my way of honoring my parents. They deserve to have the truth known about what happened. It's the last thing I can do for them."

Nicco knew he'd come down hard on Scout. What she'd been through would send many people, men and women alike, into hysterics, but she'd kept her calm and used her wits to survive.

What of next time, though? And there would be

a next time. He was certain of it. Whoever wanted her silenced wasn't going to leave it at this.

He cared what happened to her. Over and above professional interest. He'd sort that out later. Right now, he had to convince Scout to back off.

"Do you have family in another state? Aunt or uncle? Cousin?"

"My parents were both only children. Why?" A beat passed. "You want me to run. Is that it?"

"I want you to leave the investigating to me. I'll see this through. That's a promise." He didn't make promises easily, but those he made, he kept. "Being a hotshot reporter isn't worth your life."

"You think that's what this is all about? My reputation? Do you know how much I want to say yes?" She didn't give him time to answer. "But I'm not running. If I did, I'd never be able to trust myself again."

"Sometimes running is the smart thing to do."

"Would you? If you were me, would you cut and run?"

She had him there. "No."

"Then why are you asking me to do it?"

He didn't have an answer, at least not one she would accept.

"I'm scared. Right down to my toes." That caught him by surprise.

"I know something about being afraid."

She raised a brow. "You? You've never been afraid a day in your life."

"That's where you're wrong. I was scared plenty when I was overseas. Anyone who's been in combat and says he wasn't is either lying or a fool."

"Do you dream about that time?"

"Yeah. Sometimes I wake up in a cold sweat. But the dreams don't last forever, and I start again." Nicco cupped her shoulders. "When you're scared, you can come to me."

The shaking started then, followed by harsh sobs. He watched helplessly as the tears came, noisy, messy ones that tore at his heart. When she raised her head, her eyes were those of a small child who had tried her best to put up a brave front but could no longer keep up the pretense.

He stood, pulled her up and then to him, where he pressed her head against his chest. "It's all right." He said the words over and over until the trembling and crying gradually subsided.

She pushed away from him. "Your shirt's all wet."

"Doesn't matter," he said and brought his mouth to hers.

The kiss was barely more than a brush of lips, a fleeting caress. She leaned into it. Or he thought she did. How was he supposed to know? He could only guess at her reaction. As for himself, it reached inside of him and awakened something that had lain dormant for too long.

Scout remained silent for so long that he wondered if she'd been offended by the kiss. Or maybe she was angry. He'd grown up with sisters, but he was as clueless as the next man in understanding a woman.

"That was nice." She appeared to be testing the word on her lips. "Nice and sweet."

Nice and sweet. No man, no Ranger, wanted his kisses to be described in such a way, but a glance at the soft expression in her eyes made him think that maybe *nice* and *sweet* weren't so bad after all.

Involvement with a client spelled trouble, he reminded himself, as memories of Ruth intruded. She hadn't been a client, but he had been charged with protecting her. And it had led to disaster.

He refused to put a name to what he felt for Scout. Losing his heart again would mean losing parts of himself, including his ability to make rational decisions, and he couldn't afford that. The price was too high. Last time it had cost him both the woman he loved and his faith. If he hadn't allowed his feelings for Ruth to cloud his judgment, she might still be alive, along with the two men from his unit.

TEN

Scout sensed the change, both in Nicco and in their relationship. When he suggested they order in Chinese food, she agreed. Over fried rice, egg rolls and chicken and broccoli, she shared stories of her work on the paper.

Nicco's interest had her opening up in unfamiliar but not unpleasant ways. He laughed at her description of an irate mother who had called the paper when her son's name wasn't mentioned in a story covering a local science fair. With a start, she realized she was flirting with Nicco.

Her heart did a funny little flip-flop at the warmth in his gaze as it rested on her. It felt good, this tingly sense of awareness, even the jitter of nerves she experienced whenever she was with him. More, it felt right. *He* felt right.

"Sometimes I miss my parents so much that it's a physical ache. They wanted so much for me." The wistfulness in her voice, along with her unintentional change of subject, sent a spasm of pain through her. She'd been talking about her work. Why had she brought up her parents?

The answer came swiftly. Because she knew they would have liked Nicco.

Tears filled her eyes. "I'm sorry. Sometimes my emotions get the better of me."

"It's okay," he said and reached across the table for her hand. "You loved them. That love hasn't died."

"Thank you for saying that. Not everyone understands."

She thought of what she'd just shared. Talking about the loss of her parents didn't come easily. How could it? She'd bared her heart to Nicco, exposing the struggles of her soul to accept the unacceptable when her parents had been taken from her so cruelly, and letting him in on her fears. Giving voice to them had been incredibly difficult.

Not even with Olivia had she ever been so open and certainly not with Bradley, who she instinctively knew would have mocked her feelings. Nicco confused her. That was the trouble with opening herself up emotionally: she no longer had control over her feelings. Control was vital.

Despite her tenuous hold on her emotions, she risked sharing one of the most important tenets of her life. "I think trusting that God loves us is incredibly simple and incredibly hard at the same time. When we were children, most of us were taught that He loves us because he's our Father, but when we grow up and look at all the evil and pain in the world, we start to wonder. We live in a fallen world where people betray those they claim to love, where lies and deceit are so common that we start to ignore them."

"How do you reconcile the two?" Nicco sounded like he really wanted to know.

"I remember that God is there for me whenever I need Him. I have only to turn to Him. That's why He's given us the most precious gift of all—prayer."

"You make it sound pretty convincing."

"It's what's kept me going the last year." She weighed the wisdom of continuing. They were treading into the quicksand of her past, and at the same time sharing her most intimate feelings for the Lord. The combination made her vulnerable. And though she was all too aware of her fragility in this area, she was reluctant to allow others to witness it.

So why was she considering going there with Nicco? He wasn't a believer, and they had little in common, except for a need to find the truth. Was that enough? She didn't know.

"There is no other relationship as perfect as that we can have with God because He is perfect. If the relationship's not perfect, we know where the fault lies." Her voice turned husky as love for the Lord welled up inside of her. She couldn't talk about Him without her feelings spilling over.

Tears stung her eyes. She reached up to wipe them away when Nicco caught her hand. "Don't. Don't be ashamed of your tears."

"I'm not ashamed of the tears, but…"

"But what?"

"I don't want you to think I'm weak."

"You? Weak? You're the strongest woman I know, outside of my mother."

She was unbearably touched, knowing how he felt about his mother.

It was time to lighten things up. "I never thought to be having dinner with an Army Ranger. The guys at the paper are going to want details."

"What are you going to tell them?"

"That Nicco Santonni is a real-life hero." To her dismay, that didn't elicit the smile she'd expected. Instead, shadows filled his eyes. "I'm sorry. Did I say something wrong?"

"It's okay. But I'm no hero, Scout. Don't make me out to be one." The order only made her more curious than ever about him.

She put a stop to that train of thought before it could go anywhere. Bradley had stripped away her ability to trust. He'd left her without so much as a goodbye, just when she had needed him most.

It hurt too much to love someone and to lose them. Just as she'd lost her parents.

"I never expected to meet someone like you," she said, then flushed when she realized she'd spoken her thoughts aloud.

"You mean a man who knocks you to the ground and then falls on top of you."

"A man who saved my life."

"It's a life worth saving."

In going after a story, she was tough, fearless, but flirting left her feeling like a sailor who'd wandered into unchartered waters. She wasn't any good at it. Her last experience with flirting had been with her fiancé, and she'd failed miserably at being coquettish.

Relationships were foreign territory.

Since her parents' deaths and her fiancé's desertion, she'd guarded her independence. Her friendship with Olivia was the exception to keeping to herself. She was a loner and liked it that way. She wasn't exactly lonely, but sometimes she craved the company of a man who understood her. She looked sideways at Nicco, and a bunch of messy emotions flittered just below the surface.

Nicco Santonni was nudging her self-imposed independence aside, forcing her to lean on him in ways that were not only unfamiliar but downright uncomfortable. She wanted to tell him to back off, to leave her to aloneness, but she couldn't bring herself to do so. At the same time, she wanted to see where this was heading.

Everything she'd protected so fiercely in the last year was in jeopardy. Losing her parents and then her fiancé had sent her into a spiral. It was only after acknowledging that she'd never loved Bradley and was better off without him, that she admitted what she'd known from the start. He had been something to cling to.

As though Nicco knew where her thoughts had landed, he said, "Tell me about the no-good fiancé."

The description had her smiling, despite that painful time in her life. "When my parents were killed, I took a bullet to the shoulder and spent some time in the hospital. Bradley and I were casual acquaintances through work. He was a TV journalist. When I got out of the hospital, he looked me up. I was flattered. He was a well-known anchor, and I had just published my first story for the city beat."

"What was his angle?"

Her smile broadened. "You have him pegged. He wanted an exclusive about my parents' murders. Of course I didn't know that. Not at first. He was always making plans, talking about going to New York and getting an anchor seat with one of the networks. All he needed, he said, was the right story, and wouldn't it be great if he could tell my story on the news.

"I fell for it. Hook, line and sinker. When he asked me to marry him, I was convinced it was love. In fairness, it wasn't all his fault. I was looking for something, someone to take the place of what I'd lost." She grimaced. "He told my story on the news, made me sound like some pathetic victim. It received attention from the networks in New York, just as he'd intended."

"He used you."

"Yeah. Looking back, I can see that. But I had stars in my eyes and couldn't see beyond their sparkle. When he left for New York without me, I knew I'd been conned."

"Good riddance."

"He had the nerve to text me—text, mind you, not call—and ask for his ring back."

"What'd you do?"

"I sold it and gave the money to a no-kill animal shelter. Bradley hated animals. I sent him the receipt and told him he could write it off as a tax deduction."

Nicco laughed long and hard. "Good for you."

She pushed her plate back. "I've been doing all the talking. Tell me about you. What's important to you? What makes Nicco Santonni who and what he is?" The questions were ones she'd asked people she interviewed, but, with Nicco, they took on new meaning.

Nicco understood that Scout genuinely wanted to learn more about him. That was only one of the things that he liked about her, her ability to listen. Along with her desire to help others, her generosity of spirit, her unfailing courage.

He understood the significance of what had just happened, not just the revelations themselves but the act of sharing. As though aware that she'd given away parts of herself, she went silent. Her eyes, though, spoke volumes of pain and grief and bewilderment.

For all that she'd endured, she was a remarkably composed woman. There was a quietness to her, a stillness. He appreciated the restful quality she carried with her. There was nothing restful about her articles, he reflected, and a small smile worked its way across his mouth. They were pointed, even fiery, in their indictment of corrupt officials and practices. The woman wrote with a passion that was a match to her spirit.

She believed in justice and truth and all the things that so many thought naive. What's more, she wasn't ashamed of those beliefs.

"Are you all right?" He brushed his hand over her arm, and she flinched at the contact.

"Of course."

Her chin lifted, a signal that pity wouldn't be welcome. A flash of brightness gleamed in her eyes, tears that, with only a blink, were banished by sheer force of will. As unmoved as she tried to appear, this woman was still scarred by unbearable loss and unspeakable pain.

He wanted to wipe the sadness from her eyes, to lift the burden from those slender shoulders. All he could offer was his own shoulder. With a flash of insight, he realized that they were both carrying a festering grief.

Scout sat back, prepared to listen. Just when she believed that Nicco was about to share something important, glass shattered and smoke filled the kitchen.

Nicco dove toward Scout, grabbed her hand, and pulled her across the room and out the back door. There, he pushed her to the ground behind some shrubbery. "Stay down."

She struggled to process what was happening. Someone must have thrown a smoke bomb into her house to get her outside where she would be more vulnerable. The first shot rang out, perilously close to where she crouched.

With the bushes as cover, Nicco returned fire.

A volley of shots pierced the night, the bullets exploding around her. She thought she heard someone shout, but she couldn't be certain because of the pulse of terror in her ears. The smell of damp earth filled her nostrils. Head down, she wrapped her arms around her knees. Like that would help if a bullet found her.

A sob swelled in her throat. She pushed it back before it erupted, then did the only thing she could. She prayed.

When a few minutes passed with no more gunfire, Nicco crawled out and stood.

Scout remained huddled behind the shrubs. Sirens sounded in the distance.

A hand gripped her shoulder. A scream formed in her throat before she heard Nicco's voice. "Someone's called the police. I'm going to contact Detective Wagner. I want him in on this."

By the time Wagner and several patrol officers arrived, Scout had managed to pull herself together. Sort of.

"We'll canvass the neighborhood," Wagner said, "find out if anyone saw anything, but I don't expect much. When people hear gunfire, they tend to take cover." Turning his attention to Scout, the detective said, "Someone's right mad at you."

She didn't trust herself to speak and only nodded.

"Tomorrow morning will be soon enough to give your statements at the station." He included both Scout and Nicco in his glance.

"We'll be there," Nicco promised.

"In the meantime, I suggest you stay with a friend or at a motel for the night. The smoke will clear out eventually, but you don't want to stay here."

Scout packed a toothbrush, some sweats, and a change of clothes for tomorrow. They all bore the acrid odor of smoke, but no more than what she was already wearing.

"Let's go," Nicco urged. "You're falling-down tired."

She didn't argue.

He drove to a motel not far from the freeway. "I've stayed here before when I have a witness who has to lie low. It's not fancy, but it's clean."

She was too weary to answer and waited while he registered.

Nicco led the way to their rooms, checked out hers before she entered, then crossed the room to the adjoining door. "I'll leave the door ajar. Anything spooks you, yell."

"Th...th..." She couldn't get the words out.

Nicco drew her to him and held her for a long moment. "It's all right to be scared."

She pulled back, swiped at her eyes with the back of her hand. "I'm not scared." Well, she was. But mostly she was angry. Furious, actually.

"I'm getting tired of being target practice for some lowlife. If whoever's behind this expects me to run, he's in for a big disappointment." Because she was more determined than ever to get at the truth.

ELEVEN

Nicco regarded Scout with a mix of admiration and concern. She didn't back down—he ought to know—and she'd go after the truth no matter the danger. While he applauded her resolve, he worried that she didn't seem to understand just how close they'd come to dying tonight.

If the shooter's bullet had come even a hair closer, Scout would be lying on a slab in the morgue right about now.

Her steadfastness was one of the things he respected about her, but on the battlefield, arrogance could prove fatal.

He'd seen buddies who believed they were invincible mowed down by a spray of bullets that did not discriminate between courage and foolhardiness.

He sat in the room's one chair and pulled her onto his lap. She was so tiny that it was no hardship to hold her. Beneath the smell of smoke, the scent of some flowery shampoo drifted from her hair.

"It's all right. We'll get through this." He tightened his arms around her. "You need some sleep."

"I can't sleep," she said. "Not after this." She drew back a few inches so that her face was tilted to his. "Before…everything…you were going to tell me something."

Nicco didn't spend a lot of time in the past. Remembering took him down a rabbit hole that had no escape, but maybe sharing those memories with Scout would help both of them.

"An order came down to pick up a reporter at the local command post. I fought against it, saying it jeopardized the operation, but nobody paid any attention.

"Turns out the reporter was okay. Smart and savvy and pretty, a lot like you." He thought of Ruth, her intelligence, her integrity. Against his better judgment, he'd been drawn to her, and the attraction was returned. Pretty soon, the two of them were sharing smiles and small jokes. "We started talking about a future.

"And then it happened."

"What?" So immersed was he in the pain-filled memories, Scout's voice reached him as though from a great distance.

"Things hadn't gone the way they were planned…" *And when had they ever?* "…and the asset was still with us, rather than being exfiltrated. There were rumors that our camp would be raided by an insurgent group wanting to take him out. I knew I had to get Ruth out of there and sent her, along with two of my unit for protection, back to headquarters. We didn't know until it was too late that the road they'd taken was riddled with IEDs."

He told the story without any inflection, repeating it by rote. That was the only way he could get through it.

The steady hum of the room's AC unit provided background noise for the recitation of facts.

"An IED went off, killing Ruth and my men." Grief had consumed him, scraping at his heart with razor-sharp teeth.

He'd witnessed death before. Few soldiers in a combat zone remained untouched by the useless waste of life that was war. But Ruth's had reached down deep and squeezed the life from him.

"You loved her, but she's not gone. Not really. She's in your thoughts..." Scout gestured to his heart "...and in here."

"Sometimes I can't remember things about her. Her voice. Why don't I have a recording of her voice? I'd give anything to hear it again."

"You'll remember when the time is right. When you need to hear it."

"How do you know?"

"Because that's the way it is with my parents. Just when I think the memories of my mother's voice or how my father smelled of peppermint are gone forever, I remember. I tuck it away. Later, I can take it out and hold it to my heart. Then I remember how much they loved each other. How much they loved me. It's one of the Lord's tender mercies." Her voice cracked on the last.

"I appreciate what you're trying to do, but you don't get it. You weren't responsible for your parents' deaths. If not for me, Ruth would still be alive."

"You can't believe that."

"She was in my care." Bitterness clung to every syllable. "I was responsible for her and for the men assigned to me. Two good men died because of me, because of a decision I made."

He couldn't forgive himself. Neither could he forget. After he'd returned to the States, he'd gone to see the families of the two men who died. In a swirl of barbed-edged memories, he recalled the awkward meetings with the grief-stricken families. They hadn't blamed him, but neither had they wanted to stay in touch.

Why would they? He was a reminder of all they had lost.

"I started acting stupid. Taking risks." The stew of grief and guilt deepened as he recalled the risks he'd taken that endangered not only himself but the men under him. When he finally accepted the inevitable, he knew it was time—past time—that he resigned his commission.

Nicco stopped abruptly, wishing he could snatch back the last minutes. What had he been doing, confiding in Scout that way? He'd never shared the whole story with anyone, not even his family.

Saying the words aloud put a name to the pain he still carried. It had been better to keep it locked away. Exposing it to the light of day didn't help.

He thought of Scout's declaration of faith and his own lack of it. For him, it wasn't so much a loss of faith as it was a break of faith. Or maybe it was him who was broken. He'd felt broken inside ever since he'd returned from the Stand.

Ironically, he'd received a commendation for successfully completing the mission of securing the asset and his eventual exfiltration. With 4-stars, members of Congress and other dignitaries on a stage to honor him, Nicco had never felt less worthy in his life.

It was that event, along with the acknowledgment that he was risking his men's lives with his self-destructive behavior, that had finally prompted him to leave the Rangers. It had ripped the heart from him, but he hadn't had a choice.

What he'd believed, in the job, and, more important, in the Lord, had gotten all twisted up in his mind and soul.

The worst part was disappointing his mother. Rosa Santonni had brought her children up to believe in God and to worship Him at church whenever possible.

Nicco's refusal to set foot inside a church since his return to the States had caused her infinite heartache. He'd rather cut off an arm than cause his mother a second's distress, but he couldn't be a hypocrite and that was what attending church felt like.

Sometimes he struggled to bring up Ruth's face in his memory. How could he have forgotten? He had a photo, tattered and bent from being tucked inside his wallet for over three years, but shouldn't he be able to remember what she, the love of his life, looked like without a reminder?

If he did succeed in having romantic feelings for another woman, he would welcome them gladly, but the pain of losing Ruth and his guilt were obstacles he doubted he'd ever be able to overcome.

"There's more," Scout said, bringing him back to the here and now.

He took a moment to collect his thoughts before he began speaking. "Ever since it happened, I've been thinking a lot about good and evil. It should be white and black, yet too often we live in a world of gray. How do we know which is which?"

"The Lord tells us. When we're on the right path, He lets us know. Just as He lets us know when we're on the wrong one."

"How?" He realized he really wanted to hear her take on it.

She placed her hand on her heart. "We feel it here. If our heart is full of positive energy, we know we're on the right path. If we feel darkness, we know we're headed in the wrong direction."

"You sound very sure."

"I am. It's the only thing in this world I am sure about."

The certainty in her voice reached deep inside him and touched his heart. He understood Scout well enough to know that she didn't take such matters lightly.

"I wish I had your faith."

"All you have to do is to ask Him."

The simplicity of it caused him to wonder if he had the courage to do as she said. Could he ask the Lord for faith when his own had been MIA for so long? The ramifications of doing as she said settled in his gut like spoiled milk. If he did, then he had to live up to his part of the bargain.

He had lost an essential part of himself. Before he knew what he was doing, he was voicing his thoughts aloud.

"You don't have to stay lost," Scout said softly. "The Lord welcomes all His sheep. Especially the lost ones."

It was too much. He wasn't ready for this. He wasn't ready for her. "Enough." He quieted his voice. "Just...enough."

Scout understood all too well the hold the past could have. She had tried to break its grip too many times to remember, but it had proved stronger than she was.

The only way out of the pain was to hand it over to the Lord and to beg for His mercy. He was the one with power. Once she'd realized that, much of her burden had been lifted.

She wanted to share more of her faith in His power and mercy with Nicco, but she knew he wasn't ready to listen. Not yet. Instead, she could only pray that someday he'd be ready to hear the truth. To accept it.

When this was all over, Nicco would return to his life and she to hers. Whatever happened between them, she wished with all her heart that she could help ease the burden he carried and restore his faith.

And then she realized that it wasn't up to her. That was the Lord's privilege. She dipped her head in humility at the gentle chastisement. What had she been thinking, believing that she could fix the burdens that Nicco carried? What arrogance on her part to believe that she could do what only the Lord could accomplish.

She raised her head to meet his gaze and felt instantly foolish. Everything about him shouted independence, strength and courage. She doubted anyone looked less like they needed someone to worry over him.

He had rolled up the sleeves of his T-shirt, revealing arms ropey with muscle and sinew. He looked tough and able to handle whatever life threw his way, reminding her of the zing of attraction she'd experienced upon first meeting him.

Okay. Scratch the worry and focus on finding out who killed her parents.

Tentatively, she touched his arm. "You're a good man, Nicco Santonni. You aren't responsible for Ruth's death or those of your men any more than I am for my parents'."

"That's where you're wrong. You didn't give the order for your parents to take that road the night they were killed. I gave the order and the woman I loved and two of my men died because of it."

He shook off her hand. His voice roughened. "Still think I'm a hero?" What might have been shame crossed his face. "Sorry. I didn't mean to take it out on you. It was a long time ago. It doesn't matter."

Not so long. And it mattered very much. For all the bits and pieces of information that she had processed in the last few days about Nicco Santonni, this was by far the most important.

Because Nicco had become important. The admission gave her pause. When had that happened? More important, what did she do about it?

Bradley had dumped her with no more thought than if he'd been tossing away a used tissue. It had broken her heart; more, it had shattered her trust and her belief in herself.

"Because you didn't know that a bomb was buried in the road. You weren't to blame."

"Then who is?"

"What about the people who put the explosive there? They're the ones to blame."

She willed him to believe her. "The Lord has given you some pretty extraordinary gifts. He's given you some burdens, too. It's up to you to decide which will win out."

"What do you know about what the Lord's given me?" Resentment slashed through the words. "You don't know me. Don't know what I've seen, what I've done."

"I see the goodness in your eyes. I hear it when you talk about your family."

"The Lord turned His back on me a long time

ago." He shook his head. "No. It wasn't that long. Only three years. But it seems like an eternity."

She supposed it was an eternity when she considered that he'd been without the Lord in his life during that time.

"Are you sure?" She waited a beat. "Or did you turn your back on the Lord? He knows the truth. He knows what you're going through. He watches you go through it alone, and He weeps because you don't have to. He is the restorer of faith, the protector of the innocent. You are not alone. Not now. Not ever.

"Sometimes…sometimes it's too much to take in, the enormity of His love for us. How can it be that the Savior sacrificed everything for us and that He took our pain onto Himself?"

"You say you want to help. If that's true, leave it be. You can't change anything."

"You're right. I can't change anything. But there's Someone who can."

"Leave. It. Be."

"If that's how you want it."

"That's how I want it."

The roughness of his voice had Scout drawing back. Stiffly, she got to her feet. "I think I can sleep now," she said. "Thank you for staying with me."

"No problem." Nicco stood as well. "Like I said, yell if you need anything."

"Okay." But she knew she wouldn't.

After showering away the soot and smoke, Scout dressed in the sweats she'd brought with her.

Exhaustion pulled at her. Despite her assurance to Nicco that she could sleep, she doubted she'd be able to find any peace in closing her eyes. Too many emotions swept through her. Shock when Nicco had grabbed her hand and pulled her from the house. Fear as she'd crouched behind the bushes. Uncertainty of her feelings for the man who had become so important.

It was the last that kept her awake far into the night.

TWELVE

Over breakfast at a fast-food place the following morning, Scout felt Nicco's withdrawal.

"What's going on?" she asked when the tension between them had mounted to an unbearable level.

"I'll keep you safe, Scout.'"

No fancy speeches for Nicco Santonni. The no-thrills statement had the sound of a vow. He wasn't the type to make promises he couldn't keep, and something told her that if he did make a promise, you could count on him to walk through an inferno to make good on it.

But then she'd been wrong about a man before. Bradley was Exhibit A.

"But no more talk of God. Don't expect to change me," Nicco continued as if there'd been no pause. "God and I parted company a long time ago. I figure He's not any more anxious to change that than I am."

"That's where you're wrong."

"No more." His voice had a note of finality, and she backed off.

Probably a good thing. She wasn't looking for a relationship, especially with a man who made it clear that he had no room for the Lord in his life. The Lord's role in her life was the most important part of her being.

Given that difference, it made sense to keep Nicco at arm's length.

Yes, she was attracted to him, but her radar regarding men had proven faulty in the past. Make that dismal. She'd become engaged to her former fiancé shortly after her parents were killed and realized in retrospect that she hadn't been thinking clearly. Bradley had been a safe harbor in the worst storm of her life, and, in the end, he had used her, then abandoned her.

Why couldn't she have seen what he was? And how could she ever trust her own judgment again?

Nicco took her elbow, steered her out the door of the motel, and helped her into his truck.

A sprinkle of rain felt good against her skin. Apparently she was not the only one to appreciate it, as others shunned umbrellas and lifted their faces to the caress of the barely-there rain.

She chanced a look at Nicco, noted how the mist glistened in his inky black hair and glazed his face with a light sheen. "Admit it. You didn't like me when we met."

"I didn't know you," he corrected.

"And now?"

"And now I know that you're an amazing woman who doesn't back down even when she's threatened, even when common sense and self-preservation tell her to."

"I thought that just made me stupid."

"Not fair throwing my own words back at me."

She crossed her arms over her chest. "You said it. You own it."

"Ouch. That's harsh."

"Is it?"

"I was intrigued. That ought to count for something."

"If you say so."

"You don't give an inch, do you?"

"A girl's got to watch her back."

The precinct station didn't resemble those on television. There were no chain-smoking detectives barking out orders with guns at the ready. In fact, it resembled an efficiently run office with rows of cubicles bristling with voices meeting at the center bull pen. The air conditioner was apparently out. A fan belched sporadically, sending out the occasional puff of recycled air.

Nicco and Scout had been directed to a small office at the rear of the building where Detective Wagner asked questions. For the last twenty minutes, they'd gone through events leading up to the smoke bomb exploding in her kitchen.

"You didn't see anything or anyone?" he asked after first Nicco and then Scout recounted what had happened.

"We were too busy ducking bullets to see much," Nicco said.

"And you, Ms. McAdams?"

"I had my head buried in my knees."

Nicco eyed Scout with growing concern. The skin stretched taut across her cheekbones. Shadows beneath her eyes seemed to swallow her face.

She was holding it together, he judged, but just barely.

Wagner took them through the events of the previous night once more. Nicco understood the reason for what seemed a tedious waste of time. Witnesses frequently recalled details when they'd had time to think about things.

"I wish we had better news to report, but my officers didn't find anything. The shooter even policed his brass."

"A pro," Nicco said upon hearing that the man had picked up the spent cartridges.

The detective gave a grim nod.

Nicco stood, held out his hand. "Thanks."

Wagner shook Nicco's hand, then Scout's. "We'll keep on this, but I don't know how much further we can take it without anything more to go on."

Nicco and Scout exited the station.

"I've got to go to the office," she said.

He wanted to argue that she wasn't in any shape to go to work, but the set of her shoulders told him that she wasn't in the mood to listen. Besides, concentrating on work might help take her mind off last night.

They spent the rest of the morning at the paper where Scout worked on a story and he checked in with Shelley.

"Somebody wants to stop Scout before she finds the answers she's looking for," he said after telling Shelley about last night. "She refuses to leave it alone."

"Did you expect her to?"

"No," he admitted. But he'd hoped.

"You sound like it's personal," Shelley said softly.

At his silence, Shelley let out a long sigh. "It's like that, is it?" She didn't give him the opportunity to respond. "Stay in touch."

To Nicco's relief, Scout worked at the office for the rest of the day, and they ordered in lunch. The paper wasn't the best place to protect her, but having her remain in one place was better than having her out on the streets sniffing out a story.

She interested him far more than any woman

had since Ruth. Her independence should clash with her faith; instead, the two complemented each other in unexpected ways.

She could be quiet when the situation called for it. She could also be brash and opinionated. Both were parts of the whole. And the whole was entirely engaging. If he didn't watch himself, he could fall for her in a big way.

That wasn't on his agenda. He'd taken the job with S&J to prove to himself that he wasn't just a one-trick pony.

He'd risen through the ranks in the Army, then the Rangers. That didn't always translate into success when a soldier returned home. He'd seen too many buddies flounder after they'd left the Army. Some re-upped; others fell through the cracks and ended up on the streets.

Homeless vets were becoming more and more common. When they discovered the hard-earned skills they'd learned as soldiers weren't valued or even needed at home, they started questioning themselves and everything else.

When he realized that Scout was looking at him with concern, he pulled out of his dark thoughts. "Sorry. Went down a detour."

"Looked like a pretty dark detour." She touched his arm, her fingertips a light caress. "Want to share?"

"No. But thanks."

Why was he trying so hard to convince himself that he didn't want a relationship with her? She was courageous, intelligent and beautiful. She was also stubborn, foolhardy and, at times, infuriating.

The combination was intriguing and frustrating. Add to that the fact that she was a reporter, triggering memories of the most painful time of his life, and it made for a confusing brew of contradictory feelings.

"I'm ready to pack it in for the day," Scout said at a quarter past five. "I hope the cleaning service was able to deal with the smoke damage."

"I'll help you with anything that's left."

"Thanks."

On the ride home, they stopped for burgers and fries.

At her door, Nicco pushed her back when it opened on its own.

"Stay back."

She ignored him and followed him inside.

Weapon drawn, he scanned the front room, moving from right to left, before repeating the pattern in the dining area and the kitchen.

He took the stairs two at a time with her on his tail. "Don't come in here," he said when she reached her bedroom.

She pushed past him to see a picture of herself

and her parents stabbed to a pillow with what appeared to be a knife from her own kitchen.

"Don't you ever listen?"

She ignored that as well, too devastated by the ruined picture, one of the last taken with her parents. They all looked so happy, in blissful ignorance of the tragedy to come. "Why?" Why would someone want to desecrate that precious photo? It meant nothing to anyone else. It was meaningful only to her.

"Someone's sending you a message." The flatness in Nicco's eyes chilled her. He had switched to Ranger mode, the soldier in him coming to the forefront.

"My parents have been gone for a year. There's no reason…"

Nicco's arm curled reassuringly around her, providing something—someone—for her to hold on to. Even knowing that the Lord was always there, she sometimes longed for the comfort of human companionship.

She didn't feel alone any longer. Because of the man standing protectively at her side. Because of Nicco.

She reminded herself that the awareness between them was based on artificial circumstances, created by the danger they'd faced together. The truth was that they barely knew each other. Their relationship—if you could call it that—was not founded on reality.

Relationship. She tested the word.

Probably not the right word to describe what was simply chemistry. At most, it was a professional association. Nothing more. And the honest part of her called her a liar.

If all they had was a spark of chemistry, why was she having such a hard time convincing her heart? Because she found him more attractive than any man she'd ever met, including Bradley? Because she could fall for him in a big way if she let herself?

The admission cost her. She'd always prided herself on being her own person. If she admitted her love for Nicco, would she still be her? Or would she be only a reflection of the man?

How was she supposed to trust her feelings for a man when she'd been so abysmally wrong before? The questions swirled through her mind with harsh persistence.

And why was she thinking of all this when her house had just been broken into and a precious picture destroyed? She didn't have to look far for the answer: she was searching for something, anything, to take her mind from the destruction.

"It's not about your parents," he said, drawing her back to the present. "It's about you." His lips thinned into a hard line of resolve. His stance widened as though he were preparing to ward off an attack, but he kept his arm around her, letting her know that no one would get to her without going through him first.

She noticed he was careful not to touch anything, and she did the same.

"I'm calling the police," Nicco said, voice grim.

Scout wrapped her arms across her chest as though she could hold herself together with the simple act. Though having her home broken into wasn't as threatening as having someone try to kill her, it felt like the worst kind of invasion.

Weariness enveloped her, draining her of energy and resolve. Could she continue the investigation as she'd promised herself? Right now, she didn't know.

While the police had taken their statements, Nicco had made a decision.

Tolliver, the operative sent to replace Anderson, showed up, and Nicco explained what was going on. He couldn't leave Scout. Not tonight. She'd looked shattered.

And who could blame her? Last night, smoke had driven her from her home into a barrage of gunfire. Tonight, she'd returned home to find it violated once again.

Nicco wanted to be the one who protected her, who kept her safe, who stood between her and danger. Instinctively, he reached for her hand and drew her closer. He wanted to keep her right there, tucked safely at his side.

"I'm staying," he said to Tolliver. "I can't leave her tonight."

The agent was trained well enough not to question someone who outranked him.

When Nicco told Scout that he planned on staying the night, he pretended not to notice the relief in her eyes.

"I'll make up the living room sofa for you." She went upstairs, returned within a few minutes with a pile of bedding. Efficiently, she tucked sheets onto the sofa, then spread a lightweight throw over it. "There."

A slight smile curved her lips, the first she'd given since they'd discovered the break-in. "It may be a little on the small side for you."

He smiled in return. "I'll make do."

"Nicco? Thanks. For being here." She brushed a kiss over his jaw.

He started to tell her that he wouldn't want to be anywhere else but then thought better about it.

The sofa was made for someone Scout's size, not his own six-foot-three-inch frame. He adjusted his long body until his head rested on one arm of the sofa while his feet dangled off the other. Not the best sleeping conditions, but he'd slept in worse places. Lots worse.

In the cavernous cargo hold of military planes where canvas straps held his shoulders rigid while his head bobbed up and down from the constant turbulence. In bug-infested jungles where mud and slime oozed over his exhausted body and rain beat down with such relentless intensity that he felt as though he were trapped inside a bass drum. In the brutal cold of a cave in Afghanistan and in the unforgiving heat of an Iraqi desert.

Everything went quiet on the floor above him, but he didn't feel the sharp sense of aloneness he normally experienced in the hours between midnight and dawn.

Scout was there.

His mind shut down. Rangers, like other special forces, were taught to sleep where and when they could.

Tomorrow would come soon enough.

THIRTEEN

Just as Scout was preparing to leave for the paper the following morning, Leonard Crane called and agreed to an interview.

"Why now?" Nicco asked when she got off the phone. "You've been trying to get a one-on-one with him for weeks and he calls you today, less than twelve hours after your house has been ransacked."

"Like you said, I've been trying to get him to talk with me for weeks. Now he's given me the green light. No way am I passing this up."

Obviously unhappy, Nicco drove her to the union headquarters. He wanted to come inside with her, but she refused.

"Crane's more likely to open up if I go by myself." Before Nicco could respond, she climbed out of the truck and headed in alone.

Two armed men stood sentry at the door to Crane's office.

One opened the door, gestured that she should go in. They followed her inside.

"We meet at last." Crane didn't stand when she walked into his office. Nor did he offer his hand. Instead, he tapped his fingers against the desk, then rolled them into meaty fists.

Scout wasn't about to let herself be intimidated by the blatancy of the gesture.

He pointed to a chair across the desk from his.

She sat. "It's good of you to make the time to see me."

"'Good of you to make the time to see me,'" he repeated, mocking her polite words. Crane had a thick neck, a bulldog chest and a nose that looked like it had been broken more than once. He gave her a smile that was more fierce than friendly.

She held her ground, refusing to recoil from the hatred that glittered in his eyes.

"You wanted a sit-down, Ms. McAdams. I'm here. Sitting down with you. You got fifteen minutes and then you're out of here. Garbage don't wait for no man. Or woman."

She returned the smile with one as fierce as his. "I appreciate your time, Mr. Crane."

"Lennie. Everybody calls me Lennie."

If he thought his good ol' boy routine would charm her into forgetting her mission, he was doomed to disappointment.

"You're a busy man. I get it. Now tell me why

the union is making noises that it's going to walk any day now?" Though talk of a strike was bandied about, she doubted it would come to that. The city fathers understood that if the sanitation union walked out, it would cripple the city. They'd cave before it came to that.

She started with what was common knowledge, union/management negotiations, an ongoing matter. By opening with that, she hoped to disarm him before she broached what she really wanted to talk about.

"Fairness, missy. Pure and simple fairness. We've been working our tails off and for what?" Before she could answer, he jumped in. "Nothing. Nothing at all. Our wages have been at a standstill for the last five years. Our benefits have been cut. Does that seem fair to you?"

"The recession has hit a lot of industries," she said neutrally.

Crane made a rude sound. "This ain't due to no recession. Money that rightfully belongs to our people is going to greasing palms."

"Would yours be one of those palms getting greased, Mr. Crane?"

The man's eyebrows beetled, making him look like a grossly overgrown bug. "No, ma'am. They wouldn't. And I don't take kindly to people making remarks like that."

"I apologize. But you can't deny that service

has been disrupted and your men have made no secret that they want someone to blame."

"Only natural. A man looks for somebody to blame if he can't put food on the table for his wife and babies when their bellies are hungry."

She gave a short nod. She couldn't fault men for wanting to feed their families.

"Maybe those men are looking your way. And maybe that's got you nervous, making you look for someone to blame, as well." She let that settle in. "Word is that you could stop the strike if you wanted." She waited another beat. "But you don't."

"Ain't you heard a word I said? The men need to be able to feed their families. So, no, ma'am, I won't try to stop the strike if it comes to that. I stand by my men. They stand by me."

"No one wins if your men walk."

"Maybe. Maybe not. But the city will sit up and pay attention when the stink gets too bad. We'll see who blinks first when the garbage starts piling up."

She'd had enough of talking about strikes and leaned forward, folded her arms on the desk. "Why don't we get down to why you really called me here?"

"You don't waste any time, do you?"

"I never saw the point."

To her surprise, he gave a belly laugh that

shook his massive frame. "I like you, McAdams. I didn't expect I would, but I like you a lot."

"I'll try not to let it turn my head."

Another laugh. "You've got guts. I'll give you that."

"I'll take that as a compliment. Now can we get back to why I'm here?"

His face, a moment ago folded into jovial lines, now grew hard. "You're not here to talk about negotiations. You know it. I know it. You got something in your craw, spit it out."

"Okay. There've been four murders in the union over the last few years. What do you know about them?"

Instead of answering directly, he let his gaze rake over her. "You put me in mind of your mother. She asked the same questions."

Scout forced herself not to react to the mention of her mother. "And what did you say to her?"

"Same thing I'm gonna tell you."

"What would that be?"

"Curiosity killed the cat."

The threat wasn't implied. It had been direct and to the point. "You aren't stupid. Taking me out won't stop the story and you know that. Sooner or later, someone's going to discover the truth."

The sigh he let out was resigned. "I'm tired of this. What's more, I'm tired of you." He nodded to the men who had escorted her inside and had waited by the door.

"Wait." She held up a hand in protest. "You haven't given me anything."

"You got more than you deserve and all you're gonna get. Now get out of here before I forget that I'm a gentleman."

She snorted at that. "I don't frighten easy, Mr. Crane."

"Well, maybe you should."

"I think you're running scared. What's going to happen if it gets out that you've been talking to me? This story's not going away," she said as she gathered up her things. "Whether I tell it or someone else does, it's going to be told. If I were you, I'd watch my back."

Preparing to leave, she dared ask one more question. "What do you know about someone sending me threatening letters?"

"What are you talking about? I don't know nothin' about no letters."

She tended to believe him. The astonishment in his voice was too genuine to be faked.

Crane leaned across the table separating them. "You best look for a different story. This is a dirty business. In more ways than one. It cost your mama her life." He let that hang, then got to his feet "Now, I gotta be going. Some of us got work to do."

She stood as well. "This isn't over."

He rounded the desk and opened the door for them. "A friendly word of advice—if you're thinking about coming back, don't."

Nicco hadn't liked the idea of Scout meeting Crane alone, but she'd insisted. He was learning that the lady didn't take no for an answer. She didn't back down. While he admired that trait, it also made it that much more difficult to protect her.

When she reappeared less than thirty minutes later, he knew the interview hadn't gone well. Her mouth was a taut line. When he looked closer, he noted the sheen of unshed tears in her eyes.

"What did he do to you?"

"Nothing. Except saying that I reminded him of my mother and then threatening me."

Scout held him back when he would have gone inside to confront Crane. "Don't. There's nothing you can do."

"He refused to give me anything important beyond telling me that I should probably be afraid of him." Her short laugh spoke volumes.

"He's right about that. Crane's nobody to mess around with." He didn't take her straight to the paper but to a nearby park where he hoped she could burn off some of the fury that spilled from her with every breath. "Stay put."

He checked out the park. Only two mothers with children on a swing set were present. He returned to the truck and helped Scout out.

She strode from one end of the park to the other, anger vibrating from her in ever-increasing waves. The energy rolled off her. He loved the precise bridge of her nose, the strong lines of her cheekbones, the way she moved that managed to be both decisive and graceful at the same time.

He kept pace with her. "What did your gut tell you about Crane?"

"Same thing my eyes and ears did. He's crude but street smart. He all but admitted that he killed my parents or had them killed."

Finally, she plopped down on a bench. He sat beside her, slung an arm over her shoulders.

"You've done what you could. It's time to leave it to the police to find out what Crane knows."

She didn't respond to that.

They spent the rest of the morning and part of the afternoon at a community center where Scout covered another of Patrice Newtown's appearances. It was predictable fare, but the crowd ate it up. Nicco wasn't one for self-aggrandizing speeches, but he had to hand it to the woman. She knew how to play to an audience.

A trip to the paper where Scout drafted her report on the speech followed. By the time they were headed back to her place, she was dragging, and Nicco knew the morning's meeting with Crane had taken more out of her than she'd let on. She massaged the tiny space between her brows, the gesture eloquent of her weariness.

After making certain that she had something to eat, he left her to Tolliver's care and headed home for the night.

When Scout received a call the next morning after he'd rejoined her at her house, Nicco listened, frowning at what he heard.

"I'll be there. Give me an hour." She hung up. "That was Crane. He wants to meet."

Instinct kicked in. "Not happening."

"He's holed up in a hotel. He wants to make a confession and says he trusts me to make sure it gets to the right people." A noisy gulp told him she was close to tears. "He said… He said…he'd tell me who ordered the murders of my parents."

Nicco accepted that nothing would keep her from meeting the union boss. She named the hotel, and he recognized it as one with top-flight security.

Still, he gave it one last try to convince her not to go. He drew in a breath for patience. "You're bent on proving Crane is dirty and responsible for your parents' deaths. Now he calls you less than a day after you met with him, a meeting where I might remind you he threatened your life, and wants you to come to see him? It's got trap written all over it."

"He sounded scared. He said he trusted me to tell the truth. I'm going, so stand down."

Though Nicco wasn't happy about it, he accompanied Scout to the hotel.

When they reached the room number Crane had given her, they found the door ajar. Nicco went in first. "Stay back."

Leonard Crane, throat slit from ear to ear, lay on the marble floor of the classy hotel he'd chosen as his hidey-hole. At least two thousand a night, Nicco judged. He took in the half-eaten plate of caviar, the split of champagne, and mentally added another two to three hundred dollars to his original estimate.

Nicco hurried back to where Scout waited at the door, intent on telling her not to come in, but she was already pushing past him.

"You don't want to see this."

"Too late. I already have."

"Don't touch anything." He circled the body. A scrap of paper, barely visible even from that angle, extended from Crane's fingers, as though the killer had ripped a page from his grasp.

Nicco knelt, saw that the scrap held a number. Careful not to disturb anything, he copied the number in a small notebook he carried.

"Most people think that in order to slit someone's throat, you have to pull the head back, expose the neck fully." He tipped his head back, held his hand to the carotid artery. "The problem with that is the windpipe provides some measure of protection. Whoever killed Crane knew that you have to come in from an angle."

"Someone with a medical background," Scout mused aloud.

"More likely someone with military training," Nicco corrected. "Special ops soldiers are taught how to kill like that with a single slice of the knife."

He knew she wasn't a stranger to violence, had witnessed it firsthand, but he hadn't meant to paint so graphic a picture. "Sorry."

"Don't apologize. I need to know what kind of people we're up against."

His lips stretched in a hard line. "The men and women I served with would lay down their lives to protect America from her enemies, but there are always a few bad apples who use Uncle Sam's training for their own reasons."

Nicco's thoughts turned bleak, his memory calling up three members of another unit who had looted a museum in Afghanistan after it had been gutted by a mortar attack. The stolen artifacts had found their way to the black market and the men, eventually, to a federal penitentiary where they would spend twenty-plus years. At one time, they had been honorable men, good soldiers, but they'd traded their integrity for the lure of easy money.

"Once you step down into the gutter," he said after relating the story to Scout, "it's real hard to pull yourself out."

"It hurts you, doesn't it? To think that someone who served is mixed up in this."

"Yeah. It hurts. It also makes me mad as all get-out."

Though Crane had been dirty, Scout could still feel pity for him. For the wasted life that had been his. For what he might have been had not greed and a thirst for power claimed hold of him. For the violence that had taken him.

Violence left a stain. Beyond the blood that had trickled down his cheek and onto the floor in a rust-colored pool. Beyond the torn and upturned furniture. The mark could never be scrubbed away.

Given the time line of when Crane had called and when she and Nicco had arrived, he'd have been killed in the last forty-five minutes.

Nicco turned back to look at her, frowned. "You shouldn't be here."

"I've been to crime scenes before." She took a steadying breath. "Even murder ones."

"I know," he said gently. "But that doesn't mean you have to stay here. Not like this."

She wanted to take the out he was offering and get away from the ugliness, but she held fast. She wasn't running.

Nicco punched in a number on his phone. In a few terse sentences, he gave the location and victim's name. "The police are on their way," he told her, then punched in another number. "Sal, there's been a development." Nicco filled in his brother on Crane's death, then listened for a minute. "Yeah, we're sitting tight, waiting for the police to show up." He groaned. "I got it. Cooperate, play nice and tell them everything we know. Too bad they probably won't return the favor."

While they waited for the police, Nicco made a sketch of the crime scene. Scout did the same and wondered how their sketches would compare. Those drawings would prove useful when calling up details. She noted the placement of the body, the overturned furniture and other details.

The police arrived within minutes, along with crime scene technicians, the ME and others. Nicco and Scout were escorted to another room where Detective Wagner interviewed them. She judged Wagner to be a good policeman, observant, competent, committed. A blessed numbness settled over her and allowed her to answer the questions in a coherent fashion.

No, she didn't know who had killed Leonard Crane.

No, she didn't know who had reason to want him dead.

No, she hadn't seen anyone else.

And, finally, yes, she would make herself available for further questions.

Wagner asked to see the general manager of the hotel next. He nodded slightly to Nicco and Scout, a sign that they could sit in on the interview. Not that it did them much good.

The GM was unhelpful in the extreme. "This is a private hotel where our guests expect and demand the utmost privacy and respect. I cannot permit you to question them or the staff as that would disrupt the service for which our establishment is famed," a fussy man in a fussy suit told Detective Wagner, a haughty expression slathered on his face.

"It's not up to you," the detective said equably. "The sooner you let us do our job, the sooner we'll be out of your way. We can start with your staff if that makes you feel better."

Scout gave Wagner kudos for not allowing the GM to intimidate him from doing his job. She'd never had patience for those whose noses were stuck up in the stratosphere.

"Thanks for letting us stick around," Nicco said to Wagner after the detective had interviewed members of the staff.

"It cuts both ways. You two find out anything, I expect you to let me know."

"You got it."

Outside, Nicco and Scout headed to his truck.

Inside the cab of the truck, she felt his gaze on her, warm and concerned. Though she appreciated his worry, she wasn't going to fold under the pressure. She'd made a promise to herself to see this through and she wasn't going to go back on that. In her mind, a promise was a promise, even one made to herself. Especially one made to herself.

What had Crane known and why had he been killed for it?

That was the question uppermost in Scout's mind the following day as she and Nicco sifted through crime reports and notes they'd made about the union boss. Also spread across her kitchen table were photos of the scene, courtesy of Detective Wagner.

They'd tried to make sense of the number on the scrap of paper clutched in Crane's hand but had come up with zilch and had decided a change of pace from reviewing their notes and the crime scene photos was in order.

She pressed her thumbs into the corners of her

eyes in a vain attempt to relieve the growing exhaustion that had dogged her since the discovery of Crane's body. He had sounded genuinely frightened when he'd called yesterday morning, begging her to meet him at the hotel.

What had he been afraid of? Or who?

"What if we've had it wrong from the first? What if Crane was just a patsy? He was dirty, sure. But he was only the fall guy." Her voice rose as her conviction that she was right took hold. "Think about it. Crane was the sanitation union rep. What about all the other unions in Savannah? Like the longshore workers?" Her mind raced as the implications sank in. "Whoever controls the docks controls everything. What if Crane was recruited so that whoever is behind this had access to transportation? It wouldn't take much to use the garbage trucks to transport things."

Nicco nodded. "Ninety percent of everything that goes in or out of the city goes through the docks. Drugs. Guns. Human trafficking."

"Crane was a public face. When whoever was behind this saw that we weren't backing down, they decided to make sure we focused on Crane and didn't look at anyone else. He was sacrificed to keep our attention on him and off everything else. There has to be a big endgame in sight."

"It all comes back to money."

Her nod was short. "Not just money, but power.

Greed and ego are a potent combination." And sometimes a deadly one.

Talking felt good. It kept her from thinking about how cold she felt. So cold. Colder than she had ever been since the murder of her parents. She had seen death before. Of course she had. So why was Crane's death affecting her as it was? Even after several hours, the coldness hadn't gone away. If anything, it had intensified.

The answer wasn't difficult to find. If she hadn't been investigating Crane, he might still be alive. She knew the logic didn't follow, but she couldn't shake the sense of responsibility.

"Stop it."

Nicco's words had her looking up.

"You're not responsible for what happened to Crane. He made his choices. They cost him his life."

She was no longer surprised that Nicco read her so easily. He seemed to intuitively know what she was feeling and thinking. "Maybe if I'd backed off…" She left the thought unfinished.

"It wouldn't have changed anything. Crane got mixed up in something bigger than he could handle."

"He wanted out. He sounded desperate."

"It was too late. He was a means to an end, nothing more. My guess is that whoever's behind this planned on getting rid of him long before you started investigating him."

"Thank you for that." She wanted to believe Nicco, but the feeling that she was somehow responsible for Crane's death persisted.

"The only thing we can do for him now is find the killer."

"He wasn't a good man. He wasn't particularly nice. But he didn't deserve to die like that." Her thoughts took her back to the beginning. "My mother believed he was mixed up in those murders. But what if he wasn't the one calling the shots? What if he was just a pawn?

"He was trying to cover his tracks when he came after me and then realized that I wasn't the real threat. It was the people he was working for." She sat back, considered. As theories went, it wasn't bad.

"Good. You have your fire-in-the-belly back."

"Fire-in-the-belly?"

"You were so cold. So locked away in yourself. I was afraid you'd never come out."

Fire. Yes, she guessed that was how she felt. If fire meant wanting to find justice for her parents. If fire meant anger that they'd been taken too soon. If fire meant the fear that those responsible for killing her parents and, yes, Crane, too, might never be punished.

"I'm sorry. I didn't mean to worry you."

"Worry comes with the territory."

"Territory?"

"Later. We'll talk about it later."

"What do we do?"

"We go after them."

"We don't know who they are."

"Not yet." Determination lit his eyes. "But we will. And then we'll bring them down."

A chill worked its way down her spine. She stared at him, seeing his strength. She wanted to take comfort from it, but all she felt at that moment was fear. Fear for this man who had become so important to her in a short amount of time.

Nicco had made her fight his own. If something happened to him because of her… She didn't finish the thought. She couldn't.

FOURTEEN

Nicco took Scout to a hole-in-the-wall diner where they were unlikely to be spotted.

He expected her to want to work on deciphering the number he'd copied from the scrap of paper clutched in Crane's hand.

"How did you get your name?" she asked instead.

The question startled him before he understood. She needed a respite from the horror of the last hours and obliged her with the story. "My real name is Nikodemos. It means victory of the people."

Her quizzical look invited him to share.

"Mama was diagnosed with ovarian cancer twelve weeks into her pregnancy with me. The doctors told her to end it so that she could start treatment to save her life. She refused. Six months later, I was born. She told my father that I was a victory."

"And your mother's cancer?"

"After I was born, she did four months of chemotherapy. Papa said she was sick every single day, but she never complained. When I was old enough to understand, she told me that she had been blessed with a healthy baby boy, so how could she be anything but grateful. She's been fine ever since." To his chagrin, his voice had developed a hitch. "Sorry."

"That's the most beautiful story I've ever heard." Scout placed her hand on his arm and squeezed gently.

"Mama's her children's biggest cheerleader." He smiled in memory. "When Sal and I were playing football in high school, she'd yell so loud that she drowned out the other parents. Sometimes it got embarrassing, but we never doubted that she loved us."

"Now she has a whole new generation of grandchildren to cheer for."

"I dodged a bullet there. Once my sisters started having babies, I was off the hook. Now with Sal and Olivia married and expecting, I have another reprieve."

"Is that what you want? A reprieve?"

For the first time since he'd discovered that girls were different from boys, he stammered. "Uh…well, I mean…"

Scout laughed. "You're in danger of tripping over your tongue."

He laughed as well. He couldn't help it. Something about her made him want to laugh. The laughter died in his throat as he stared at the notebook where he'd copied the number from the piece of paper clutched in Crane's hand.

Scout's gaze followed his. "Back to the real world," she said wryly.

He opened the notebook to the page containing the number. The more he tried to make sense of the sequence of digits, the more frustrated he grew. A code? The seven numbers appeared to be totally random.

Scout looked over Nicco's shoulder. "It's too short for a social security number. There're no letters so it's not a license plate. And the prefix is wrong for an area code."

"So what is it?"

"Let's go high-tech." She powered up the laptop she was never without and entered the number in a search engine.

Now it was Nicco who watched over her shoulder. When the results came back "not found," she tried again, this time separating the numbers into groups. Still no hits. "This is getting us nowhere," he said in disgust.

"Give me a minute." She tried another configuration. "Hey. I think we got something."

"What is it?"

"A warehouse number."

Nicco hadn't been expecting that, but it made sense. Once they finished lunch, they drove to the warehouse district. Located in an area that gentrification had yet to reach, the district boasted dozens of structures that ranged from renovated to dilapidated to barely standing, a section of the city the city fathers preferred to forget. A pockmarked parking lot where straggly weeds pushed their way through cracks in the concrete skirted a tired brick building.

Despair oozed from the surrounding area. Graffiti decorated the walls while broken windows yawned like giant maws. Empty bottles and trash littered the parking lot. A couple of men slunk away, their drooping shoulders and furtive eyes mute testimony that they had given up on life.

Scout looked like a hothouse flower that had been mistakenly transplanted into a weed patch. "You don't belong here." The words were out before he could stop them.

"Nobody belongs here."

He could only agree. He let himself out of the truck, came around to help her out. "Stay behind me."

She nodded.

Weapon drawn, he surveyed the outside of the building. Except for the two men who had disappeared into the shadows, it appeared deserted. What they would find inside was another matter.

The warehouse was predictably dilapidated and appeared to be abandoned. Perfect camouflage if someone was storing contraband inside. The only giveaway that all was not as it seemed was the shiny new hardware on the doors. While Scout served as lookout, Nicco picked the lock and slid the doors open.

A musty smell greeted them. Nicco peered into the darkness. An ancient forklift occupied one corner. Further inspection revealed row upon row of neatly stacked crates. Each crate bore a number, probably an inventory marking.

He discovered a crowbar propped against a wall and pried open one of the crates. What he found inside was enough to start a small war.

He did a quick count. "There's got to be forty crates of M110s here. Each holds six dozen. At several thousand dollars each, that's…" He did some rough-and-ready math in his head. "Sold on the open market, these will bring a couple million dollars. Easy.

"Probably more," he said, amending his own calculation after further inspection. "These are prime Army issue." He pulled a pair of latex gloves that he routinely kept in his back pocket and lifted a weapon from the crate, held it in ready position. The sleek weapon could kill a dozen people in less than a minute.

Nicco thought of the gun left behind at the fund-raiser, no doubt part of this shipment. It was all coming together and painting a very ugly picture. Military weapons sold on the black market commanded a premium.

"That's what this whole thing has been about. Transportation via union trucks. The murders. All to move thousands of weapons." Nicco's lips tightened as he thought of the misery the semiautomatics could inflict if they fell into the wrong hands, whether gangs in the States or terrorists abroad.

He pried open another box, this one a different size, and found a dozen .50 caliber sniper rifles. With the Browning AP, the armor-piercing weapon could blast through steel plate.

A final box yielded an AT-4. The three-foot disposable fiberglass tube could fire a six-and-a-half-pound projectile through eleven inches of armor. It could wipe out anything from the presidential limousine to an Abrams tank. It was one of the deadliest of the weapons in the warehouse. Nicco had seen an AT-4 in action. The devastation it had wreaked was forever imprinted on his mind.

Silently, he gestured for Scout to take a look.

"How did the Army not know?" he wondered

aloud. "They've got someone on the inside. No other way it works." He made a rude noise. "One of our own. If I get my hands on him…"

After 9/11, Nicco had enlisted with the ideal of "Never again." Never again would America's enemies be able to invade his country and slaughter thousands of people, innocent civilians who had done nothing to warrant such hatred.

Like many young soldiers, he saw the world in terms of black and white. Black was evil and needed to be eradicated from the face of the earth. White was pure and just. Some men wore black hats; some wore white. He saw himself as one of the white hats.

Experience had shifted his viewpoint until he sometimes wasn't at all certain of what was black and what was white. War had a tendency of painting events and people in shades of gray.

He'd struggled to understand the real difference between good and evil, beyond the assumptions of the naive boy he'd been. Recognizing those differences while serving his country had made him who he was today, a man colored by his experiences, many good, a few not so good.

The idea that someone in the military had used his or her position to facilitate the theft of weapons sent anger spiraling through him.

"This changes everything." His gaze locked with hers. "This isn't just about union murders any longer. Someone wants to start a war. You're out of this. As of now."

No sooner were the words out of his mouth than a barrage of fire hit the warehouse. Rage burned through Nicco even as he forced his racing thoughts to slow. He needed to think, not react. His and Scout's lives depended on how he handled the next few minutes.

He pushed her down. "Keep low."

"Any lower and I'd be a snake's belly," she muttered.

Another woman might have given way to cries of fear, but not Scout. She kept her head.

"We're going to get out of this."

"Never doubted it. What's the plan?"

He wished he had one. "Thinking on it."

"Think fast."

"We need to split up. I'll distract them while you go out the window."

"Not happening."

"We don't have time to argue." He'd calculated the rounds of fire, the spacing between them, the distance from their origin. "There're at least four tangos. That makes four guns to one."

"Give me your clutch piece. I'm licensed to carry." He looked at her doubtfully.

"Don't sell me short, Ranger."

"You're full of surprises." He withdrew the Sig Sauer strapped to his ankle. "You any good?"

"I hold my own." The breath she drew sounded shaky, but her hands were steady as she checked the clip.

"Okay. Can you keep them occupied while I work my way behind them? If I can pick off one or two, it'll even things up."

"Watch me."

Nicco wanted to believe she was as good as she said she was. He had to. "Let's do it."

Per her shooting instructor, Scout held the weapon in a two-handed grip that gave her the most control. At Nicco's signal, she let loose a steady stream of fire out one of the broken windows, hoping that the shots would give Nicco the most protection while at the same time distracting the gunmen.

Just before he left, he winked, the jaunty gesture doing much to bolster her spirits. Out of the corner of her eye, she saw him make his move, keeping low to the ground.

A thud. The sound of a shot finding its target. One down, she mentally ticked off. Three to go. She checked her clip. She'd have to reload after another two rounds.

A shout pierced the air, causing her to flinch. She refused to let it rattle her. She had a job to do. Nicco's life was at stake as well as her own.

She fired off her last two shots, then replaced

the clip, fumbling as she did so. The delay cost her valuable seconds. More rapid-paced fire. She listened intently, trying to distinguish between Nicco's gun and that of other weapons. A grunt reverberated, then the slap of flesh against flesh. It had gotten down to hand-to-hand combat now.

What did she do? With her gun freshly loaded, she could continue firing off rounds, but would that help Nicco? She held her weapon at the ready and headed in the direction of the fight.

FIFTEEN

Nicco finished securing the remaining assailant with zip ties. Three men were down, the fourth had escaped. He called first 911, then Sal, and listened as Sal told him about weapons stolen from an Army arsenal last year. "You think these are the stolen weapons?" Nicco asked.

"It makes sense. I'm going to make a few calls, see if we can get the Army to send someone to check it out." Sal clicked off.

Scout joined Nicco just as he was finishing up the conversation. "What? You saved all the fun for yourself?" she asked and handed his Sig Sauer back to him. He replaced it in the ankle holster.

What a woman.

"You handled yourself like a pro," he said. "Why don't you carry a gun of your own if you have the license?"

"After my parents were killed, I promised myself I would never be a victim again. I worked out, trained at a dojo, and took shooting lessons.

But when it came down to carrying a weapon... I couldn't. I kept remembering the sound of the shots, the smell of cordite."

Something stirred in his chest when she squared her shoulders. Scout was a fighter. Most people would have run when confronted with machine-gun-toting bad guys. Not Scout.

Sirens screeched in the distance, and two police cars slid to a stop outside the warehouse. Wagner climbed out of an unmarked car and walked toward them.

"You two attract trouble like my grandma's blueberry pies attract flies." The detective shook his head, whether in admiration or resignation, it was hard to tell. "How'd you come upon this?"

Nicco took the detective through the steps that had brought them to the warehouse when he noticed that Scout was sagging.

His arm across her shoulders, he walked her to where he'd parked the truck. Her legs had started to shake, along with the rest of her, and he helped her inside.

"Will you be all right here for a few minutes?" he asked. "I need to finish up with Wagner."

"Sure. I just need to sit down before my legs give out."

"You were terrific back there."

Warmth suffused her. She wanted to discount it as the result of the adrenaline-charged events of the last hour, but she couldn't deny her pleasure at his words. He walked a short distance away, and she saw him making some calls.

"Okay," Scout said when Nicco returned. "What's happening?"

"Sal said that weapons were stolen from an Army arsenal last year. He thinks we may have stumbled on them." Before she could process that, he asked, "What do you know about militias?"

"You mean, outside of George Washington's militia in the Revolutionary War?"

A rich chuckle. "Yeah."

"Not much." Her brow wrinkled as she struggled to understand what militias had to do with Crane's murder.

And then she got it. "Transportation. The militia needs transportation to move the weapons. Enter Crane and the union."

"Bingo."

"You said the weapons were stolen last year. This had to have been in the works for at least that long."

"I had another talk with Sal, who referred me to a contact in the Army Criminal Investigation Command. The guy said that the Army's been trying to find these weapons for the last year, but whoever was behind the theft kept moving them. He speculated that the People's Militia was getting bids from all over the world before trying to sell them, after the militia takes what they want, of course. They'll be shipped wherever there's a war going on or wherever someone wants to start a war."

"How do you know it was the People's Militia who stole the weapons?"

"One of our operatives looked into the group last year." Nicco hesitated. "The militia killed his little brother. He's been tracking them ever since, trying to get a handle on them."

She shuddered at the idea of thousands of weapons being in the wrong hands. She'd covered enough shootings to understand, at least a little, the misery that such a large number of weapons would inflict. The death toll would be astronomical.

"If those weapons had reached the black market, there's nothing that would stop the violence." Nicco's voice was grim, a reminder that he'd witnessed massacres. When his cell rang, he picked up the call, listened. "Thanks, brother." He turned back to Scout.

"That was Sal. He called a contact in the DOD. MPs have been assigned to guard the weapons until they can be transferred to a secure location."

Wagner got back to them then. "Looks like you've been busy," he said to Nicco. "I just got a call from my boss's boss. Says we're to stand down and let the boys in green take over."

"Sorry about that, but the Army's got a big stake in this."

"You don't have to convince me." Wagner shifted his gaze between Nicco and Scout. "I know you folks have got to be beat. Go home. If there are questions, we can take care of them later."

Nicco took her home, where she changed into soft cotton sweats. Though the temperature hovered in the high 80s, she was cold and welcomed the cup of tea he made for her. When her hands trembled so badly that she couldn't hold the cup, he took it from her.

"It'll be all right," he murmured and lowered his head.

The kiss was infinitely sweet, and she felt herself melting into it. She returned it with a quiet fervor she'd never felt with Bradley. For a second, she wondered if she were simply responding to the stress of an emotionally-charged day, but realized that her feelings for Nicco were the real thing.

That was something she'd have to think long and hard about.

Nicco worked it out in his mind. He'd put it to Scout logically, rationally, sanely. He'd keep his totally illogical, irrational and insane fear for her out of it.

She was a smart woman. She'd see that he

was right. He hoped. After they'd returned to her place and she'd cleaned up, she'd been her usual confident self, but he'd detected the hint of vulnerability beneath the fierce pride and independence.

Worry was fruitless, but it didn't stop him from worrying over her. She'd gotten under his skin and was quickly finding her way deeper inside. He could fall into the sweetness of her touch, the smoky depths of her eyes, and lose himself there.

That was a problem for another day. For now, he needed to keep his focus sharp. That meant concentrating on the job, in addition to making her realize that the mission she'd set for herself—finding her parents' killer—had turned into something bigger and far more dangerous than she'd anticipated.

Scout was savvy and smart, but she was also stubborn, believing she could handle anything that came her way.

Whoever had killed Crane and was behind the theft of the weapons was totally ruthless. If Scout had come up against him, she would have pitted herself against a man without remorse or conscience.

Nicco was brought up short by his thoughts. Why had he automatically assumed that it was a man behind the corruption and murder? He'd witnessed enough in his time in Afghanistan to know that women could be equally deadly. Perhaps even more so than men because society still liked to believe that women were the weaker sex.

There was nothing weak about Scout. She was one of the strongest individuals—male or female—he knew. But she wasn't invincible. No one was.

He had the opportunity to bring up the subject when he arrived early the following morning to take his shift.

The scent of frying bacon and…was it real maple syrup?…reached him. Bacon and waffles. He quickened his step.

Tolliver met him at the door.

"How is she?" Nicco asked.

"All right. Considering."

Nicco didn't have to ask, *Considering what?* Crane's murder and a warehouse full of stolen weapons, plus being fired at by automatic weapons, took *considering* to a whole new level.

"Stay," Nicco said when the man would have taken off. "Maybe you can help me convince her to back off and let the professionals handle this."

Tolliver shot Nicco a you've-got-to-be-kidding look, but nodded. Together, they walked through the small front room to the kitchen.

Nicco sniffed appreciatively. "Something smells good."

Scout looked up from where she was tending

a cast iron skillet filled with strips of thickly cut bacon.

His stomach responded predictably with a growl. "Sorry about that."

She waved off his apology. "Good. You're hungry."

"Starved."

Scout folded her arms and offered a simple blessing over the food. Her praying no longer made him uncomfortable.

They shared the breakfast of bacon, waffles rich with real maple syrup, and orange juice. She snagged a strip of bacon from his plate, sending him a mischievous smile as she did so.

The move struck him as somehow oddly intimate, as well as the act of eating breakfast together, elbow to elbow at the small kitchen table. Tolliver could well have been on another planet.

"What's our next move?"

The eagerness in her voice reminded Nicco that he had some fast talking to do if he wanted to convince her to back off from the investigation. He pushed away his plate and tipped his chair back so that it rested on two legs. To say what he had to say, he needed to put distance, however small, between him and Scout. "The last couple of days have been pretty intense. I was thinking you might want to take a breather."

Disappointment gathered in her eyes. "You mean step back."

"Yeah. I guess I do."

She likewise pushed her plate away, stood, her movements brisk. "We've been through this already."

"You could stay with Olivia and Sal. Olivia would love the company."

"So the little woman stays at home while the big, strong Ranger goes out to slay her dragons."

"That's not how I meant it."

She planted hands on her hips, chin lifted. He recognized her tough-girl look. Too bad the sprinkling of freckles on her nose ruined the effect.

"Isn't it? You want to stash me somewhere safe, somewhere I won't get in your way."

He slammed his chair forward, the sound reverberating through the kitchen. "I want to keep you safe. Keep you alive." He sent a look of appeal to Tolliver, who made a show of cutting his waffle into small bites.

"I have to do this, Nicco. I can't stop. Not now. Not when I'm so close. And I am close. I can feel it."

"If something happened to you…"

"It won't. Not with you at my side."

Her faith in him humbled him. Awed him. Terrified him.

"Don't make me choose between you and what

I have to do." She touched his arm. "I'll obey orders. Do whatever you say. But don't ask me to back away from this. I can't."

He had a feeling that things were going to come to a head in a short time. It was up to him to keep Scout safe. If he failed at that, nothing else mattered.

Scout had said what she had to. And now she waited.

Nicco held her gaze with his own. "Whoever's behind this murdered Crane. Just like he murdered your..." He stopped.

"My parents. Don't you see why I can't back away? I'm sorry about Crane. He was a sleaze, but he didn't deserve what happened to him. He deserves justice. Just like my parents."

"I don't want the same happening to you." He reached across the table to take her hands in his. "You matter. A lot."

Her heart softened at that, but she wasn't backing down. If Nicco thought she would, then he didn't know her. Maybe it was time they had this out. Right here. Right now.

"I'm not running. Not now. Not ever. That's not who I am." Her eyes begged him to accept that. To accept her.

"Don't you get it? These people are playing for keeps."

"Don't you get it?" She threw his words back at him. "I'm in too deep to pull out. Whoever is behind this is running scared. That gives me the advantage." Her voice hardened. "I'll gut it out on my own if I have to." She waited a beat. "But I'd rather have you with me."

Scout waited for his agreement, but it didn't come. She withdrew her hands from his. She knew that Nicco was trying to protect her and at the same time deal with the unpalatable reality that someone in the military was using his or her position to facilitate the sale of thousands of stolen weapons. He was torn. She got that, but she couldn't allow him to dictate to her.

He got to his feet.

She stood toe-to-toe with him. Unwilling to back off. Unable to back down. "I know you're worried, but that can't make a difference. I'm in this for the long haul."

"I'm trying to save your life. That means you sit the rest of this out."

Angry heat crawled all over her at the order. "And I'm trying to find out who murdered my parents." Her sigh came heavily. "We've been through this before. I know you want to protect me, but I can't stop. Not now. Not when I'm so close to the truth. If you care about me, you won't try to stop me."

Breath hissed between his teeth. "If I care

about you… I'm trying to make sure that I never cause another woman's death."

Her heart bled at the anguish in his tone. No words she could say would convince him that he hadn't caused Ruth's death. Only the Lord could do that. At the same time, she had to stand up for herself or she risked losing the essence of who she was.

"I'm sorry about Ruth. I truly am. But I'm not her." Scout pointed to herself. "This is who I am. If it's not to your liking, maybe you should take a step back."

"Is that what you want?"

The storm clouds gathering in his eyes warned her to back off, but she couldn't. Not about this.

"The better question is, is it what *you* want?" Tears glistened in her eyes. She balled her fists to wipe them away. "I think we need a break. Another agent can take over my protection detail when Tolliver goes off duty. If you want to fix what you just broke, you'll find me at the paper. If not, well, I'll have your answer."

She gathered up her purse, her laptop, and walked out of the house with Tolliver. The uneasy look he threw her way told her he'd been acutely uncomfortable witnessing the confrontation between her and Nicco.

When Scout walked into the newspaper office twenty minutes later, she was called over by Delia, the secretary who kept everything running.

"Hey, Scout, I heard about Crane's murder. Are you all right?"

"Fine." The lie must have been reflected in her eyes for Delia raised a brow.

"Really?"

"I'll be okay." Right now, it wasn't Crane's murder that upset her. The order Nicco had issued still caused her to see red. They'd argued at other times about her backing off the investigation, but they'd managed to work it out. Why had this time been different?

Perhaps this last incident had been so intense because she'd thought he understood how important this was to her. Obviously, she'd been wrong. Just as she'd been wrong about Bradley. She was really batting a thousand when it came to men. Bradley had wanted to use her, Nicco to control her. She wouldn't tolerate either.

After an uncertain glance in Scout's direction, Delia took off. To her chagrin, Scout had forgotten the other woman's presence. Scout knew she'd handled it poorly and promised herself she'd make it up to her friend.

Feeling raw and uncertain, she kneaded the space between her brows, something she realized she'd been doing a lot lately. For the first time in a long time, she didn't know where she was going.

Then she remembered her promise to herself to find the truth. Because truth mattered.

It always mattered. Truth was inconvenient. It was messy. It created problems as much as it solved them. But it mattered. She'd built her life upon that. If she abandoned it now, she might as well throw away everything else she held dear.

Truth mattered. It had to be told.

And, so, she'd tell it. But what was the truth?

SIXTEEN

A relief agent had shown up at the paper, taking over for Tolliver.

Scout bit her lip. Guilt lapped at her conscience at her reaction to Nicco's suggestion that she back away from the investigation. He had only been trying to protect her, and she'd thrown it back at him. Even as she tried to convince herself of that, anger wove its destructive path through her as she recalled his high-handed orders.

She punched in his number. "We need to talk. I'm at the paper."

"I'll be there."

When he showed up at the office fifteen minutes later, it was all she could do not to throw herself at him.

They both spoke at once. "I'm sorry—"

She gave a sheepish smile. "You go first."

"I was wrong to try to exclude you from the investigation."

"And I should have understood that you just wanted to keep me safe."

The words, freighted with meaning, were right on both their parts, but the tension beneath them told her that a huge chasm still separated them.

Would they find a way to bridge it?

After a brief explanation, Nicco dismissed the operative sent to take his place. The man looked like he wanted to argue but accepted the orders from a senior agent.

The drawn lines in Scout's face told Nicco that they hadn't resolved what stood between them. They'd patched things over, but that was only temporary, like a cheap bandage that could peel away at any time.

He knew he'd been in the wrong, trying to force Scout out of the investigation. He'd been clumsy and insensitive because...because why? How did he make her understand his feelings when he didn't even understand them himself?

And so he concentrated on what he did best. The job. He was overdue for checking in with Shelley and gave her a call, putting the phone on speaker so that Scout could listen in. "Scout's on the line, too."

"You hanging in there, Scout?" Shelley asked.

"Doing my best." Nicco couldn't help noticing that her voice sounded ragged.

After he explained the connection to the People's Militia, Shelley said, "I'm sending someone who knows the group inside and out."

"Ransom." Nicco waited a beat. Another. "Are you sure he's ready? He was pretty broken up."

Mace Ransom, former Ranger, had good reason to want in on the takedown of anyone related to the People's Militia. When he was serving his country overseas, his younger brother joined the militia, believing he'd be serving his country like his big brother. The brother, Troy, only eighteen, had died on one of the militia's raids.

"It's been a year," Shelley said. "Mace needs to do this. And you need to let him."

"I get it."

"Mace has good instincts. Use them. He won't let you down."

"I know that. Ransom is solid as they come."

A baby's wail interrupted whatever Shelley had been about to say next. "Hold on." Within seconds, soothing sounds replaced the cries. "Okay. The IP address you gave me is anonymized."

Though Nicco knew his way around a computer, he was by no means a whiz at it as Shelley was.

"Without going into a bunch of computer-ese, I traced an account to an LLC with an address on the Isle of Man."

Things began to click into place. Apparently

they did for Scout as well. "The Isle of Man has one of the most secure offshore trust jurisdictions in the world. It rivals Switzerland in terms of privacy."

"That's right," Shelley said. "It's nearly impossible to get past the shield and find out who's behind the limited liability company."

"But?" Nicco prompted, knowing she had more. Shelley wasn't one to give up. The more impossible the problem, the more she dug in until she found the answer.

"I'll keep digging."

"Great. Thanks, boss. I owe you one."

When Scout's phone rang, she reached for it, still trying to get a handle on what she'd learned. She found an unfamiliar voice on the other end. "Scout McAdams?"

"Yes."

"Bug told me how I was to call you if something happened to him. Iffin' you was still alive." A giggle punctuated that.

"I'm still alive." Apparently the dryness of her tone reached him for he gave another little giggle.

"Yeah, I guess you is, at that."

"What did Bug want you to tell me?"

"He left something with me, somethin' I was to give you."

Her pulse quickened. "What is it?"

"A little stick." The caller sounded puzzled. "Nothin' to make such a fuss about, but Bug was real anxious that I get it to you."

"A memory drive."

"Yeah. Guess so."

"Tell me where you are. I'll come to you."

She disconnected the call and filled in Nicco.

"There's no way of talking you out of going, so I won't even try," he said.

"Thank you."

They met Bug's friend in a fast-food place, and he gave her the drive as promised.

"Why are you doing this?" she asked.

"Bug was a friend," he said simply and slunk off without ever giving her his name.

Nicco took her home, and they got to work.

"This is what Bug planned on giving me," she said, "until he decided to turn on me instead." A momentary sadness caught in her throat. "If only his greed hadn't gotten the better of him, he might still be alive."

"Giving the drive to his friend was his insurance policy."

To her surprise, Bug's information didn't start with Crane but with Patrice Newtown. Scout's interest quickened as she read further.

If Scout was interpreting the records correctly, Newtown had been using the charity her husband had started to cover up multiple transfers of money to Crane.

Scout's lips tightened at the hypocrisy of it. She'd been wary of Newtown from the start, but had allowed the woman's professed desire to help Savannah's poor cloud her judgment.

The charity's corporation was a blind for its real purpose, creating dozens of shell businesses to make it as hard as possible to tie a single person to the core enterprise. Each business bore a different name—yet another way to blur the truth—but they all shared the same address, a PO box. Whoever had set up the shell companies probably didn't think anyone would get this far.

Digging deeper into what Bug had discovered, she found what she was looking for, the final link between Crane and Newtown. It was buried under multiple layers and lawyer-ese, but once she knew where to look, it wasn't all that hard to find.

Everything became clear.

The two were in each others' pockets, the socialite and union boss. Between them, they controlled most of the city's infrastructure. There was no telling how many cops and city officials were on the take.

She felt Nicco looking over her shoulder.

"It makes a terrible kind of sense, using her charity as a front, doesn't it?" Scout asked. "Even the sanitation union fits in, providing the trucks necessary for moving the inventory."

"Newtown's smarter than anyone gave her credit for," Nicco agreed.

Scout nodded, her thoughts swirling. The flaw-less manners and gracious façade masked the woman's true character. The queen of Savannah society, the lady who gave so generously to the homeless and poor, was a common crook.

When the Newtown money had run out, she wasn't about to give up the lifestyle she enjoyed. Or the opportunity to play Lady Bountiful to all those who worshipped and adored her.

"Gotcha," Scout said as she stared at the columns of numbers.

Math had never been one of her strengths. She'd struggled through college algebra, calculus and statistics. The more she studied the spread-sheet, the more the numbers blurred before her eyes. She needed a break and a fresh perspective.

"Can you make sense of it?" she asked Nicco.

"A little. There are layers. Layers upon layers, distancing Newtown from the dirty business of gunrunning."

Scout printed out what she needed and, with Nicco, went to see Daniels. He needed to know the truth about Newtown.

She found him in his office behind his desk, as usual, but that was where *usual* ended. He'd kicked his wardrobe up a notch or two, and his gray hair sported a salon style rather than his normal barbershop special.

Scout had always admired him. The man had made no pretense of having come from the wrong side of the tracks. The antiquated expression, which had all but disappeared from popular lexicon, still held true when it came to distinguishing between blue bloods and commoners in the privileged Savannah society.

One of the city's nouveau riche, Daniels was regarded as an upstart in the eyes of the ruling elite.

A self-made millionaire, he hadn't let that stop him from pushing his way in. He had literally bought his acceptance into the upper echelons. Enough money could polish over the rough edges of poor beginnings, especially if that money was thrown at approved charities and the arts. Daniels had always made certain his money went to the right causes.

Upon seeing Nicco, Daniels scowled. "What's he doing here?"

Scout made the introductions. "There've been some incidents," she said, choosing her words carefully. "Nicco's keeping an eye on me." Wanting to defuse the tension that vibrated between the two men, she gave an admiring whistle. "Looking good, boss."

Color stained his cheeks. "Thanks." The gruff

word held both embarrassment and pleasure. "Trying a new look for tonight's party."

The gala. With all that had been happening, Scout had totally forgotten the event.

"You'll be there." Daniels made it an order.

She ignored that. When he saw what she planned to show him, he'd forget about tonight's festivities as well.

All business now, she laid out what she had. "You see it, don't you? There's a pattern. Money into the charity, and, a few days later, an equal amount is filtered out. It's labeled different things, but it disappears." She tapped a finger on another piece of paper. "And look at the corresponding payments to Crane."

Daniels glanced at the papers, then pushed them aside. "Crane's dead. What difference does it make?"

She couldn't believe she'd heard correctly. "What difference? Of course it makes a difference. Newtown was paying off Crane to move the weapons when the time came."

Small lines of disbelief puckered Daniels's brow. "I hope you don't expect me to believe that Patrice Newtown is stealing from her own charity and involved in gunrunning. We'd be the laughingstock of the city, the whole state, if we ran a story like that."

He steepled his fingers and speared Scout with

a hard look. "Do you have any proof? Any proof at all besides a few transfers of funds?" The contempt in his voice caused her to flinch.

She felt Nicco stiffen beside her and laid a hand on his arm, knowing he wanted to come to her defense at her boss's tone. Daniels was accustomed to doing the intimidating, rather than the other way around.

His voice was the rumble of nearby thunder warning of an impending storm. It originated from a thick chest that had probably once been muscle but had long since gone to fat where arms as big around as logs used in a fireplace were folded.

She knew from past experience that he wasn't above using his size to intimidate others, though she'd never known him to be violent.

He was a big man with an ego to match. She'd never held that against him, believing that ego was tempered by intelligence and integrity. Now she wondered.

"I don't have proof. Yet." The admission came hard. "But it makes sense. Think about it. Where else is she getting her money? And why the payments to Crane if they weren't payment in advance for moving the stolen weapons?" She let that sink in. "She's class all the way, and Crane was barely more than a union thug."

"So she was slumming." But it was a weak an-

swer, and they both knew it. "Get your proof."
He bent over the desk, a clear sign of dismissal.
"Now, if you'll excuse me. I've got work to do.
The paper won't put itself out, you know."

Salon-styled hair. Placing a froufrou event over
a real news story. Ordering her to drop a story
that could rock Savannah's conservative under-
pinnings. None of it was like Daniels. Not like
him at all.

Come to think of it, there were a lot of things
that weren't like him lately, especially his order
that she cover Newtown's charity events.

Scout hadn't known what she'd expected from
her boss but certainly something more than this.
A few years ago, he'd have jumped at the possibility of such a story. Now he'd brushed it off as
though he couldn't be bothered.

Was age slowing him down? Or was there
something more?

More than a few rumors were floating around
that the paper was losing money as more and
more readers canceled their subscriptions in favor
of getting their news online, but the paper was
only one of Daniels's holdings. Even if it went
belly-up, the man still had more money than he
could spend in ten lifetimes.

A photograph of two young men in college
football uniforms snagged her attention, their
arms slung around each other's shoulders.

Scrawled at the bottom of the photo were the names *Beef and Lennie*. She remembered Daniels telling her once that he'd been called *Beef* by his teammates.

She looked more closely at the second man. Leonard Crane? When Daniels received a text on his phone and answered it, she shifted her gaze to Nicco, then redirected it to the picture.

The slight nod he gave in return told her he understood the significance of the photograph.

Daniels looked up. "Was there something more, McAdams?"

"No, sir." Deflated, she left the office and wondered what her next move was.

She knew with absolute certainty that Newtown was dirty, but she still didn't have any definitive proof. The numbers showed a pattern, but that was a long way from having enough evidence to arrest the society maven, much less to convict her.

What was she going to do now? Crane was dead, so were the leads she'd dug up on him. It seemed that she was dead in the water wherever she turned.

SEVENTEEN

"You saw it. Daniels and Crane." Scout's voice rose in excitement, then ended on a dejected sigh. "But it doesn't prove anything."

"No. But it's interesting." Nicco had been weighing the possibilities. "You know Daniels. Would he be involved in something like murder and gunrunning?"

"I didn't think so, but now… I don't know. You heard him. He didn't want me following up on the connection between Crane and Newtown. Now I'm wondering why."

Nicco steered the truck toward his place. Mace Ransom was meeting them there.

Nicco glanced at Scout's profile. Strong, yet with a soft cast to the features.

Though they'd put aside their argument from this morning, things were stiffly awkward between them, their words guarded. They were working alongside each other, but they weren't together. Too much separated them.

His fault, Nicco thought. He knew what finding the truth behind her parents' murders meant to her, but he'd dismissed its importance without taking into account the intensity of her feelings. Now they were both paying the price for his stupidity.

When Mace Ransom showed up at Nicco's house, he looked around, nodded. "You're making something good here."

Nicco recalled that Scout had said much the same thing. He made short work of the introductions. Any other time, he'd have enjoyed catching up with Mace, who had been one of the best Rangers in his unit and was now a top operative for S&J.

But he and Mace had work to do, going through the invoices S&J had obtained from the Army on the weapons stolen a year ago and comparing that to the list of weapons seized from the warehouse. He glanced at Scout, saw that she was already on her laptop, probably ferreting out further connections between Crane and Newtown.

"Let's get to it," he said to Mace. With both ex-Delta and ex-Ranger operatives on the payroll, S&J had close contacts with the military and maintained good relations with most of the branches. He gestured to the hard copies of the reports. Though he had electronic copies, he preferred working from paper. "Take a look."

Mace settled on the dumpy sofa, squared one leg over the other, and read, turning the pages in seconds. His speed-reading abilities were well known among S&J operatives.

"You two have stumbled on one of the biggest robberies in Army history." Mace's low whistle echoed Nicco's own fury. The weapons represented millions of dollars, and even more, they spelled suffering and death for untold numbers of people.

"It's a massive haul," Mace continued, his eyes cold. "These weapons get out and we'll be counting bodies in the thousands, the tens of thousands."

Nicco didn't have to hear the numbers spelled out. He bit his inner cheek as he thought of the misery these guns would inflict upon innocents. The death toll of the military weapons getting into the wrong hands could be astronomical.

Scout looked up from her laptop. "Nicco told me a little about the People's Militia. You think they're behind the theft of the weapons?"

"Oh, yeah." Mace's features twisted with grief and anger. "The Army has their weapons back, but the militia members who took them are still out there. This stops here. Now."

Nicco couldn't agree more.

Scout figured that she could get in a good four hours of work before having to get dressed for the night's doings. Her lips curled in disgust at the idea of having to attend a party to honor Patrice Newtown.

While Nicco and Mace continued to pore over Army invoices, Scout got to work on finding definitive proof that Newtown had been involved with Crane.

Her thoughts strayed back to her background search on Newtown and the discovery of her sister's name, Irene Kruise. The name had struck a chord then as it did now. Scout silently berated herself. If she hadn't been so rattled by the attempts on her life, she'd have made the connection sooner.

Wanting to verify it, she entered Kruise's name in a search engine. The computer brought up a grisly story of murder and corruption.

Three years ago, Irene and Alfred Kruise had been convicted of the murders of a federal prosecutor, his wife, and two US Marshals, as well as three counts of attempted murder. They were currently serving twenty-five-year consecutive sentences on each charge.

Now Scout knew why the Kruise name was so familiar. Shelley Rabb had been hired to protect the son of the murdered prosecutor and, in doing so, had met Caleb Judd, the boy's uncle. The three of them had nearly been killed by the

Kruises. The story had a happy ending, bringing Shelley, Caleb and his nephew together.

A tingling awareness told Scout she was on to something. She called Nicco's attention to what she'd discovered about Newtown. "She's Irene Kruise's sister."

His expression turned dark. "Maybe murder runs in the family."

Scout wasn't surprised that he was familiar with Kruise's name. From what Shelley had told her, everyone at S&J knew of the murderous husband-and-wife team.

Okay. So Newtown had some bad apples on her family tree. So did a lot of people. That in itself didn't make her a criminal.

Scout followed the links of Newtown's charity's website. Though her computer skills were no match for Shelley's, Scout was knowledgeable enough to navigate her way through the various sites. ISPs crossed paths with other internet service providers for similarly based charities. In addition, the charity supposedly had over a hundred employees, but she could find tax records for only two.

The rest were only ghosts, officially on the books but with little to nothing to show. A small payment here, an approved credit card there, but a paltry presence for the numbers and amounts that should have existed.

Scout scanned the list of the Board of Directors. Among the names of other city leaders was that of Gerald Daniels.

Daniels. Her publisher. Her boss. Still, it didn't mean more than that Daniels served on the charity's board. She thought of the picture she'd seen at Daniels's office and redirected her efforts. A few taps of the keyboard and she struck gold at the website of the Georgia Tech football team.

Gerald Daniels had held the coveted position of quarterback while Leonard Crane played left tackle. A definite link between the two men, yet Daniels had never mentioned knowing the other man. It would have been natural for him to say something when news broke of Crane's death, like "Yeah, I knew him back in the day." But he'd said nothing.

"Take a look at this." She showed the website to Nicco.

"A definite link." He filled in the background for Mace, who nodded.

"Why? Why keep it a secret?" Scout asked, giving voice to her thoughts. What other secrets was Daniels keeping?

"Only one reason I can think of," Nicco said. "He didn't want the connection between him and Crane made known."

She searched for a reasonable explanation for Daniels's behavior and found only one: Daniels, the publisher of the city's biggest paper, was involved in the plot with Crane and Newtown. And that meant he was also involved in her parents' deaths.

She went over the last few days. Crane's summons, the promise that he'd tell her why her parents had been killed, his own murder before she could meet with him a second time.

The stolen weapons, weapons that would have to be moved when they were sold. That meant transportation, which is where the sanitation union came in. With Crane in on the scheme, there were hundreds of trucks available.

"And Newtown and Daniels? What's in it for them?"

"Money," Nicco and Mace answered together.

With the sale of the weapons, both Newtown and Daniels would move into the ranks of billionaires. But was there ever truly enough for people who lived as they did?

Scout thought of the players. Crane, Newtown, and Daniels each brought something to the table: Crane provided the transportation, Newtown, the charity to funnel funds, and Daniels, the power to keep the press busy with trivial matters like social events and away from real news that might interfere with the trio's gunrunning and murder.

Scout, Nicco and Mace hashed it out together.

"I almost feel sorry for Leonard Crane," she said. "He was a pawn."

"And, like a pawn," Nicco said, "he was sacrificed when the time was right."

Scout drew herself up, stretched after being hunched over the computer. "We're going to get the evidence that proves that Newtown and Daniels are dirty right up to their salon-styled hair."

Nicco grinned. "That's my girl."

For a moment, she forgot the angry words they'd thrown at each other and her hurt at his refusal to understand why the investigation was so important to her. All she heard was the warm approval in his voice.

"Can you see Patrice Newtown in lockup?" She laughed at the image.

Any trace of laughter vanished, though, at what the woman had done. It was one thing to play hardball in business, another to use a charity as a blind to cover her criminal activities, including trafficking stolen weapons and murder.

Working in conjunction with the militia, Newtown and Daniels were operating an empire built on greed, corruption and murder. An empire Scout planned to topple. "She's going down," Scout said with quiet determination. "She's going down hard."

Before Nicco and Mace could react, Scout received a call. The name on the display showed it was from Daniels.

"Scout, I owe you an apology for earlier," he said. "I wonder if you could meet me at my house in a half hour. There are some things I need to tell you."

Was he going to confess?

"I can do that. See you then."

She related Daniels's part of the conversation to Nicco and Mace.

Predictably, Nicco shook his head. "No way are you going to his place."

"Wrong. No way am I not going." She winced at the hard note in her voice and worked to soften it. "This is our chance to learn the truth. I have to go." She waited for his reaction. Would he understand? Or would he try to force her to the sidelines as he had that morning?

Nicco looked like he wanted to argue, then nodded abruptly. "We go together," he said, and waited a beat. "Or not at all."

She lifted her gaze to his, saw the rock-hard determination that matched her own in his eyes. "Together."

He turned to Mace. "Keep working the inventory."

"You got it."

Outside, when Nicco started for his truck, she

shook her head. "He's expecting me to come alone. That means I drive."

They stopped by her house so she could pick up the tickets for the night's gala. Tension filled the car as she drove out of the city. It ratcheted up several more notches when Nicco objected to her going inside Daniels's home by herself.

"He's more likely to talk with me alone," she said. "We want proof he's involved. If this is how we get it, then I have to do this."

The highway twisted and turned, a lazy river, flanked by lush fields where leggy thoroughbreds frolicked, each worth ten times more than the home where she'd grown up. *The rich are different from you and me.* F. Scott Fitzgerald's words were never more true.

Money had been never a priority for Scout. Family and faith came first. Always had. Always would.

She had no problem with those who worked hard and earned what they had. It was those who stole, who embezzled, who threatened and murdered to get their riches that had her hackles rising.

The road had narrowed now, a further sign of wealth. It signaled to one and all that this was a private drive leading to a very private house. She ignored the crushed oyster shell driveway flanked by lush flower beds, which she knew from previous visits led to a fountain at the front entrance. She steered the car to the back of the estate and pulled to a stop.

Nicco rolled out of the car in one smooth motion. "I should go with you," he said before she drove away.

"We've been over this. And if things go wrong... I'm going to need you on the outside where you can move freely. I'll call you in a half hour. If I don't..." She didn't finish. She didn't have to.

"Nicco..." She let her eyes say what her lips couldn't. "Be safe."

EIGHTEEN

Nicco wiped his hands against his cargo pants as he squinted to see through the darkening shadows.

The Daniels estate sprawled over hundreds of acres. Famed for its antebellum origins, it had the reputation of being a showplace. He wished he had an idea of the layout of the grounds, of spots where snipers might be placed, of security measures.

With the Rangers, he'd often relied on HUMINT. Human intelligence was considered the most reliable by the military. While analysts could speculate and hypothesize what might happen in any given situation, having someone on the ground was far preferable.

But he didn't have that advantage now.

He had performed countless missions, his hands dry, his heartbeat steady. Now his palms were wet, his heart racing. He could smell his own stink, the stink of fear. It oozed from every pore. For a man who had fought and, yes, killed for his country, fearless in the most dire circumstances, it was a rude awakening to discover that he was as human as the next.

He'd failed to protect Ruth when she'd needed him. What made him think he'd do any better the second time around? He thought of Scout and her unflinching courage. It was one of the reasons he loved her as he did. It also terrified him. Because he loved her.

She knew him inside and out. She knew about the scars he would always bear because of Ruth and the two men who'd died on his watch. With quiet understanding, she saw beyond all the barriers he'd put up to the raw wounds beneath and then ignored them to offer him grace.

He'd shared his deepest secrets with her, some he hadn't even confided in his family. He rationalized that with the thought that he didn't want to burden his parents and his brothers and sisters with the pain he bore, but the honest part of his brain mocked the lie.

It was Scout, and only Scout. Scout who saw through his carefully constructed defenses. Scout who, with only a touch, managed to soothe away long-held pain. Scout who gave of herself so easily that she wasn't even aware of it.

He'd let her down when he ordered her off the case. He wouldn't let her down again.

* * *

Gerald Daniels looked down at where Scout was bound to a chair.

Despite her best efforts to mask her suspicions, he'd seen through her. Less than five minutes after she'd been escorted into the walnut paneled library, he had ordered two men, the same two who had attacked Nicco and Scout in the alley, to tape her to a chair.

"Back at the office, I was afraid you'd put it together. I saw it in your face. You saw the picture. Me and Lennie. I should've gotten rid of it years ago, but that was the game where we won the state championship.

"You knew what it meant."

She gave up the pretense of not understanding the picture's significance. "You and Crane. I didn't want to believe that you were involved, but you were in it the whole time."

"Of course I was. I like you, Scout. Always have. That was why I tried to warn you, to make you see sense and give up the story. But you were as stubborn as always."

"You tried to have me killed."

"If I'd wanted you dead, you'd be dead already." The bald statement was given without any apology. "The shooting, the beams falling, the thugs trying to take you out—Crane was responsible for those. He never could do anything right. I sent the letters to you to warn you away. Why didn't you listen? We could have avoided all this if you had paid attention, but, no, you had to keep investigating."

Scout felt disgust settle in the place of disbelief. "You have to know you won't get away with this." She winced at the hackneyed words. She was a writer. Couldn't she come up with something more original?

Apparently Daniels thought so as well for he made a tsking sound. "That's pathetic."

Inwardly, she agreed, but she kept her chin raised. "I'm not the only one who knows about you."

"Who else have you told?"

She didn't answer that. "Why don't you let me go and we'll go to the authorities together?" It was a desperate ploy, one she didn't expect to work. She was stalling. Daniels knew it, too.

"Your material needs work." His laugh was full of derision. "I knew a Girl Scout like you wouldn't back off. I gave you fair warning, and you chose to ignore it."

"How can you do this?"

For the first time, regret moved into Daniels's eyes. "I have to look out for number one."

Scout stared at him. The callousness of the statement shouldn't have shocked her, but it did.

She'd been deceived in the worst way possible. Keep him talking.

"Why? Why all this? Why throw away everything?"

"The oldest reason in history. Money. Lots and lots of money."

"You have more money than you'll ever spend."

"There's never enough money."

"When did it happen? Deciding to chuck everything you ever believed in and become someone you don't even recognize?"

"You're a fool. You know that, right?"

"A fool because I wanted the truth? Isn't that the paper's motto?"

"A naive fool," Daniels continued as if she hadn't interrupted. "Truth can be shaped. It can be finessed to say whatever I want it to say. It can even be bought. The way I see it, I can buy myself a whole lot of truth with one sweet operation."

Instead of feeling triumphant or even satisfied that her suspicions about Daniels had been confirmed, she felt only an unbearable sadness. She looked at him now and saw a man betrayed by his own weakness.

"The way I see it, you sold your soul. And for what? Money you don't need?"

"Survival. The paper's bleeding money. Why do you think I haven't hired any new reporters in over a year?"

She knew the paper was losing money. She also knew he had more than enough funds to keep the paper afloat, but she played along. "If things are so bad, how are you keeping it going?"

"A nice big cash influx from a private party."

That made sense when she remembered one of his maxims: never use your own money when you could use someone else's. Despite his wealth, Daniels was notoriously cheap, both in his personal and professional life. The office joke was that he would steal the bark from a dog if he could find a way.

"Let me guess who that private party is. Patrice Newtown."

Consternation darkened his eyes. "Like you say, you're guessing."

"Am I? Those papers I brought you? They told the story. From there, it didn't take much to figure out that Newtown was in cahoots with Crane. The only one I wasn't sure about was you."

"Now you know."

"Now I know." But there was no triumph in her words, only regret.

"Then there's Christine." The plaintive note in Daniels's tone snagged Scout's attention.

"What about her?" Scout had met Daniels's wife, Christine, at a Christmas party and thought her a nice if ineffectual woman.

"Christine's an addict. Has been for years. I

tried my best to get her into a rehab program, but couldn't find one that didn't make my skin crawl. Newtown's connections let me get her into a first-class place."

"I'm sorry. For her. And for you. But that doesn't excuse what you've done. What you plan to do." She gentled her voice. "There are other ways to help her. Ways that don't involve murder."

"What would you know about it? You ever loved someone who's an addict?"

Scout sympathized with his situation, but something in his tone rang false. He was lying to her even now. She looked for any glimpse of the man she'd known for five years and saw only a stranger. Even if the paper failed, he had money and power aplenty, but it wasn't enough.

Though Scout went silent, her mind was churning. Appealing to her onetime friendship with Daniels hadn't worked, but that didn't mean she was beaten. She'd survived witnessing the murder of her parents. She'd survive this as well.

"You really think she's going to split it with you. Newtown is used to calling the shots."

"Patrice is so wrapped up in her own ego that she won't even notice she's been moved out. By the time she realizes she's been cut out of the deal, it'll be too late."

"You sure about that?" Newtown didn't seem

like the kind of woman to be cut out of anything. She liked to call the shots.

"For all her talk about empire-building, she's still a woman. That means she's weak. And foolish."

"I wouldn't sell Newtown short. What makes you think she'll keep you around once this is all done? You're an errand boy, nothing more. Like Crane." She let that sink in. "To think I looked up to you. I was a fool."

"You got that right."

Scout kept her head high. No way would she allow Daniels to see that she was terrified. "I'm sorry for you," she said, meaning it.

"You're the one who's tied up and waiting to die."

"I'm the one who believes in something more than myself. You'll never have that. No matter how rich you are, how much richer you'll get, you'll never know the joy that comes from believing in something bigger than yourself and from acting out of integrity instead of greed."

"Oh, I believe in something bigger than myself all right, like controlling the biggest gunrunning operation this side of the Mississippi." Daniels's left eye twitched, a tell he had often bemoaned. "And if you don't shut up right now, I'll tape your mouth shut. See how that'll feel."

"What happened?" she asked softly. "When did you lose yourself?"

And then the answer walked in.

Patrice Newtown, bandbox fresh, waved a hand in dismissal of the question. "Around the same time that he discovered the joy of having more money than he ever dreamed of."

"Looks like you took the old saying of 'charity begins at home' to heart, Duchess," Scout said.

Newtown laughed in what Scout supposed to be delight. "Gerald told me that you were quick. He was right." She let her gaze wander from Daniels to Scout and back to Daniels. "Did he tell you that tired story about needing help for Christine?" She didn't give Scout time to answer. "Christine left him as soon as she got clean. She couldn't wait to get away from him. She was repulsed by what he'd become."

Scout nodded in confirmation of her earlier suspicions that Daniels had been lying to her regarding his wife.

"Patrice…" Daniels began.

Newtown cut him off. "Go back to whatever you were doing. Ms. McAdams and I have some talking to do."

Daniels left but not without one last look at Scout. She thought she saw a hint of apology in his eyes, but it was immediately extinguished.

Newtown pressed a button at the side of the

desk and within seconds, a man appeared. She gave one short nod.

Less than a minute later, Scout heard a muffled shot followed by a thud. "You had him killed. Just like that."

"Dear old Gerald was falling apart. He barely kept it together when we had to kill Crane. He was weak. Like most men." Newtown directed a bored look at Scout. "You could have saved yourself and the rest of us a lot of trouble if you'd left it alone."

Scout ignored Newtown's taunt in favor of recalling one of her favorite scriptures and letting it echo in her mind. *Have I not commanded thee? Be strong and of a good courage; be not afraid, neither be thou dismayed: for the Lord thy God is with thee whithersoever thou goest.*

She tried to bolster her courage, but it was definitely sagging. *Lord, I'm tied up and waiting for a couple of killers to come for me. What am I supposed to do now?*

Newtown thought she was in charge. She didn't know Nicco and what he could do. More important, she didn't know what the Lord could do.

Right now, Scout was pinning her hopes on both of them.

NINETEEN

Nicco racked the slide of the Glock, clearing the chamber and checking the function before slipping in a new magazine. Going into battle, a soldier always made certain his weapon was ready for the fight.

He didn't try to fool himself. He *was* going into battle.

The HK UMP was a powerhouse of a weapon, right up there with the AK-47. He was as at home with the deadly tools as other men were with a hammer. Right now, he wished he had one—or both—at his disposal. His Glock was fine, but it didn't have the firepower to it that the larger weapons did.

Scout hadn't called him at the agreed-upon time. He could only surmise that she was in trouble.

Don't sell me short. Her words echoed in his mind, both a warning and a comfort. Her small stature notwithstanding, she was a powerhouse and she'd fight with everything she had.

"Lord, I need Your help. Scout is in trouble. I need to find her and bring her home." He paused. "Amen." The quiet words rested softly in his heart.

It was ironic, him praying to the Lord he'd determined wanted nothing to do with him. The two of them hadn't been on speaking terms in years. As Scout had pointed out, the Lord hadn't stopped believing in Nicco; Nicco had stopped believing in Him.

Nicco hadn't done anything to earn the Lord's love or His trust. He'd turned away from Him out of anger and grief. Just as that self-condemnation scourged him, Scout's words sounded in his mind. *You don't earn the Lord's love. It's a gift, freely given out of the infinite love He has for each of us.*

Could she be right? Could the Lord love a sinner such as himself? Nicco wanted desperately to believe it. Why should the Lord believe in someone who had abandoned Him as Nicco had?

Do You believe in me? The words were torn from his heart. Nicco waited, but no answer was forthcoming.

And then it happened: a quiet peace stole over him, and he realized he had his answer after all.

For the first time in years, he felt the Lord's

presence. It was as though God had wrapped him in a glow of warmth and strength from the inside out.

Lord, I believe in You, and right now, I could really use Your help. Scout needs us both.

Newtown raked Scout with a contemptuous glance. "You'll never be anything more than a second-rate reporter. This grand story you've been working on—it will die before it even gets off the ground."

"You mean the story about you, Daniels and Crane being involved in gunrunning?"

Newtown looked nonplussed. "You don't know what you're talking about."

"I know enough to make you nervous. That's why you wanted me out of the way. You were afraid I was getting too close." Scout couldn't hide her revulsion. "The weapons you stored for your friends in the militia? Do you have any idea what they'll do to the city? The country?"

"People will die. People who are too stupid to make something of themselves. A cleansing of sorts." The supreme lack of concern in Newtown's voice was as offensive as the indifferent words.

"One question. Why did you have me assigned to cover your events?" Scout thought she knew the answer but she wanted it confirmed. "Let me guess. 'Keep your friends close and your enemies closer.'"

Newtown looked pleased. "I knew you were bright. Gerald and I figured what better way to keep tabs on what you were doing than to have you under our thumbs."

"You thought of everything. Except that Crane figured out he was expendable. That's why he called me at the last minute."

"Right again."

"So you had him killed. And then it was business as usual. Mustn't let a little thing like murder get in the way."

"Crane had his uses," Patrice said. "When he'd outlived them, he was disposed of. Just like you will be."

Scout refused to flinch. She had no doubt that Newtown would do exactly as she promised. Though Scout was bound to the chair, she wasn't helpless and spit her disgust at her captor.

Newton gasped as she wiped Scout's spittle from her cheek. "I should have expected something so vulgar from the likes of you."

The blow came without warning, so vicious that it whipped Scout's head back.

She tasted blood as her teeth clamped down on her tongue. Involuntary tears sprang to her eyes. Darkness spun around her.

Newtown rubbed her hands together as though brushing away something particularly loathsome.

Scout watched as the outward layers stripped away, revealing the ugliness inside. Gone were the genteel manners and lady-like demeanor. In their place was a hard, grasping woman who would stop at nothing, including murder, to achieve her ends.

"People are disposable to you, aren't they?" Scout challenged.

"Of course." Newtown lifted one slender shoulder in an elegant little shrug. "Murder has been with us since Caine killed Abel. It's a necessary part of life. It always will be. I took care of Crane and Daniels just as I took care of Edmund."

At Scout's gasp, Newton smiled. "Didn't know that, did you? My dear husband had run the Newtown fortune into the ground. If I hadn't mixed a dose of digitalis with his heart medicine, he'd still be spending money on his charity like it was water, wasting it on a bunch of people who weren't fit to breathe the same air I do."

"You killed your husband?" Scout worked to take it in. Newtown's revelation stunned her.

"Of course. He was already under a doctor's care for a heart condition. When his heart gave out, thanks to a little help from me, there was no reason to think he hadn't died of natural causes. No autopsy. Of course, I played the part of the devoted widow to perfection. I must say I looked spectacular in mourning black. You're shocked, aren't you? You shouldn't be. Edmund was giving away our fortune faster than the accountants could keep up with his stupidity. And now Daniels wanted to edge me out."

Each was as much a victim of the woman's greed as Scout would be if she didn't find a way out of this.

"They deserved to die," Newtown finished.

Scout listened to the woman's rationalization of cold-blooded murder. Despair threatened to take a chokehold as she realized that Newtown would dispose of her with the same callous disregard for life. She fought against it. She couldn't afford to give way to it, not if she wanted to survive. "You're making a big mistake."

Newtown had started to walk away but now stopped, turned back to Scout. "What mistake?"

"If you kill me, Nicco will come after you like fury," Scout said with cold certainty. "There's no place you can hide, no place that you can run where he won't find you and bring you down." She had no doubt of that.

"I'm counting on it."

Scout stopped breathing. "What do you mean?"

"Did you think I didn't know he's here? Gerald's security system has been recording him since you dropped him off at the back of the estate." A satisfied smirk twisted Newtown's mouth. "Your boyfriend will come for you, and he'll discover a nice little surprise I'll have waiting for him."

Fear crawled up Scout's throat. "Please...you have me. Isn't that enough?"

"No, it isn't. I don't let people who have crossed me go unpunished. And you and the Ranger have caused me plenty of trouble. You could have dropped the investigation at any time, but you didn't."

"So you're going to kill Nicco out of spite, is that it?"

"I would never be so childish. I'm going to kill him because I can."

Scout's stomach crumpled in on itself, and she bit down on her rising despair. Giving in to it wouldn't help Nicco. She went quiet. *Dear Lord, I know that You are in charge. Please protect Nicco. He doesn't deserve to die because of me.*

She looked up to find Newtown staring at her. "Praying?" Her features contorted in contempt.

"You wouldn't understand."

"You're right."

Newton looked down her patrician nose at Scout. "It looks like we've come to the final act."

TWENTY

Newtown pushed a button on the desk once again, summoning the same two heavily armed men.

Newtown flicked a glance at Scout. "You know what to do with her."

"You want us to kill another one," the larger of the men said, "that'll cost extra."

"Are you hard of hearing?" The pleasant tone contrasted with the hard gleam in Newtown's eyes. "If so, I can find someone whose hearing is better and who knows how to obey orders."

The man shrank under the lash of her words. "No need for that. No need at all."

"I didn't think so." She spared one last look at Scout. "You'll have to excuse me. I have a party to get ready for. Too bad you won't be there to cover it. I'll look stunning, of course. I'm wearing Versace." With that, Newtown took herself off.

The two men strapped a vest fitted with explosives to Scout. So this was the surprise Newtown had referred to.

Scout did her best to squash the panic that bubbled up inside of her, temporarily turning her brain to mush. *Don't give in to it. You're smarter than that.* The pep talk could only take her so far, though. She had to think and think fast.

"Why are you doing this? Newtown can't be paying you enough to commit murder."

"Ain't like I haven't done worse," he said conversationally. His accent placed him in the backwater region of the state that had remained largely unchanged for the last hundred or so years.

He was clearly hired muscle. She wouldn't get anywhere trying to talk with him, so she clamped her lips shut and started plotting how she could free herself. Her options were slim, and the possibilities of getting out of here looked bleak at best.

She didn't doubt that Nicco was coming for her, but that could mean his death. For the first time since the ordeal began, she prayed that he wouldn't find her in time.

She'd never thought to care deeply for a man again, but love had found a way. What she'd felt for Bradley paled in comparison to what she felt for Nicco. Now it may well be too late.

She squared her shoulders as much as she was able and reminded herself that she was used to going it alone. That wasn't right. She'd never been alone.

The Lord had always been at her side. He wouldn't desert her now. She wouldn't betray her faith in Him by giving way to fear.

"Lord, I'm in trouble. I need Your care. And please watch over Nicco." She closed her prayer with a simple "Amen."

Though she was still bound to the chair and the death vest remained strapped to her, Scout felt a sense of calm overtake her and knew that the Lord was already doing His part.

Nicco looked at his hands. The sweat had dried on them, and he was once more the Ranger he had been for so many years. Training kicked in and wiped out all emotion. Normal men would experience an adrenaline rush now. Nicco was not normal. His pulse slowed to measured beats; his lungs drew in air in measured breaths.

Thank You, Lord.

He stopped, listened. And heard nothing. Where were the thugs who were undoubtedly in place and ordered to stop him?

He came to a brick-lined patio. There, dumped like so much garbage to be cleaned up by others, was Gerald Daniels, a bullet in his back.

French doors were left open, no doubt in invitation. He approached cautiously, stepped inside.

And saw Scout, hands and feet taped to the arms and legs of a chair, a vest rigged with explosives strapped to her upper body. His lips thinned at the dried blood that had formed at the corner of her mouth.

He inhaled deeply. Paralysis was threatening to take a stranglehold on his mind, his body.

His hands clenched, unclenched as he forced out the terror and concentrated on what needed to be done. He'd trained himself to recognize fear and then to use it. He'd come through plenty of hairy times, but he'd never been as terrified as he was at this moment.

Lord, I need You. The prayer never made it to his lips but settled in his heart. Stronger now, he gave Scout a confident smile.

Fear darkened Scout's eyes, but her words were calm. "The explosives on the vest are connected to the chair. If you try to free me, it'll go off and kill us both."

He'd been afraid of that. "No problem."

Her eyes told him that he hadn't fooled her. Not for a second. He didn't blame her. There was the very real possibility that he couldn't save her. The likelihood of that grew greater with every second as his gaze landed on the timer.

The vest held numerous different-colored wires. It was a common ploy of bomb-makers, an attempt to confuse anyone who tried to disarm it. Nicco wasn't intimidated by that, but the timer was a different matter. Fortunately, it hadn't yet started.

He'd seen similar things during his time with the Rangers. Whoever had done this was an expert, another sign that ex-military personnel were involved.

Nicco set about sorting the wires. After identifying which were which, he cut them systematically until the timer clicked on.

"Go, Nicco. I couldn't bear it if something happened to you."

He ignored that.

"Please…go. If you die because of me, I'll never forgive you."

Nicco couldn't find it in him to grin at the remark. He and Scout were both going to die unless he stopped the timer.

Get in, get it done, get out. The motto of his Ranger unit rang in his mind. Status of first part: done. He was in. Status of second and third: in progress. Going through the checklist steadied him.

Nicco could feel the tug of exhaustion that began to eat away at the corners of his mind, the result of unbearable stress. He shook it off. The knowledge that Scout would die if he didn't do something hit him like rounds fired from an AK-47.

Patience, he cautioned himself.

If there was one thing he'd learned as a Ranger, it was patience. Skill with weaponry, close-quarters combat, offensive driving—they could all be taught. But patience had to be won through experience. He chafed against it, but he held onto it, forcing himself to take his time.

"One of us has got to be smart," Scout said. "You're elected." Though her chin quivered, her voice was strong, and he fell in love with her all over again.

"We need to stop the timer," he said, thinking aloud. "Something to wedge against the hand." The space was a scant eighth of an inch.

Scout looked down at her necklace. "The pencil."

"Are you sure?"

"I'm sure."

Carefully, he removed the necklace from her and wedged the pencil against the timer hand. The timer stopped, buying them precious minutes.

He recalled the words of his commanding officer in EOD. *What's the first rule in bomb disposal?*

Figure out what will kill you first and what will kill you second.

Wrong. Don't get emotional over the bomb is first.

Despite his training, he was definitely getting emotional. *You think?* Seeing the woman he loved wearing a vest of explosives, yeah, he was emotional right now. Fear was a physical being, scrabbling at him with tiny, nasty claws. Okay. Put a lid on the emotions and get to work.

Second: don't look at what they want you to see. Look at what they don't want you to see.

What didn't the tangos want him to see? The trigger wire was obvious. Too obvious, and he ignored it. He flashed her a confident smile. "We go together." Or not at all.

A second trigger wire had to be there. Painstakingly, he lifted a red wire. There. Tucked in a fold in the vest, almost as an afterthought, was the second. He cut it. So far so good.

Third and final rule. You gotta believe you'll make it out.

A picture of Scout in bridal white flashed in his mind, followed by another of her pregnant with their child. They were both going to make it out of here. Alive.

He knew what he had to do.

So do it. His CO's words resounded in his mind.

"I love you," she said.

"Right back at you." More prayers took hold

in his heart. Nicco poised the wire cutter over a third and final wire. "Hold your breath."

"How long?"

"Until…" he clipped the second wire "…now."

Nothing. Only silence. Blessed silence.

"Is it done?"

"It's done." He pulled away the tape, helped her up.

"Please. Get this thing off me." Her voice trembled, echoing the one that caused her shoulders to do the same.

Carefully, he undid the vest, set it aside. He removed the pencil from the now-defunct timer and placed it around her neck.

Scout heaved out a breath and sagged against Nicco. The nerves in her hands were protesting as they woke up. She felt like a million red ants were stinging her palms and fingers.

"Here. Let me." Nicco took her hands in his and rubbed them.

The burning sensation grew worse, and she tried to pull her hands away.

"Give it a minute," he said.

He was right. Gradually, the stinging sensation subsided, and she said a silent prayer of gratitude that they were both alive.

"You did it. You cut the right wire. You saved my life. It's getting to be a habit."

"One of my better ones." His voice sobered. "When I saw you with that contraption strapped to your chest… I prayed as I'd never prayed before."

"What happened?"

"I knew that the Lord was guiding my hand. I'll never doubt Him again."

Nicco's words filled her with joy. "Deep inside, you knew He was there for you. You just needed to be reminded of it. You are a hero, Nicco, in every way."

"How do you do it?" he murmured.

"What?"

"Make me feel foolish and strong at the same time." He framed her face with his hands, and she leaned her cheek against one of the callused palms.

"Maybe because you do the same to me."

"We need to get you to the hospital, get you checked out."

"Not yet," she said. "Not until Patrice Newtown and the rest of her merry band are behind bars." She gave him a look that brooked no argument. "We're going to the party tonight. I want to make sure that the Duchess gets everything she so richly deserves."

Her brave words were cut short when the two men who had bound her to the chair appeared.

It looked like bad guys weren't done with them yet.

TWENTY-ONE

The men Nicco thought would have material-
ized earlier now made their appearance. He recognized them as the two who had attacked him
and Scout on the night they'd gone to meet Bug.

"We meet again," the larger of the men said.
And charged at Nicco.

Nicco recalled that the man had a glass jaw and
zeroed in on that. He pounded his fist into his opponent's jaw and pummeled with all his weight
until the man went down.

But he didn't stay down. He leapt to his feet and
came at Nicco, murder in his eyes. He wrapped
his arms around Nicco's neck, cutting off the
air supply. Nicco bucked, clawed, but the man's
greater weight proved to be too much.

Knowing he was in trouble, Nicco made a last-
ditch attempt to free himself. If he lost consciousness, he was as good as dead. And so was Scout.

He groped for the man's eyes. Target secured.

Nicco jammed his thumbs in the eyes. He didn't press hard enough to render the man blind, only to force him to release his hold.

A guttural cry was quickly followed by the lessening of pressure.

The man grabbed for his eyes as Nicco burrowed his shoulder into the back of the neck. With just the right pressure, he shut off the blood flow to the carotid artery. A second later, the man was out.

Scout was busy dealing with the second man.

At the man's grunt of pain, Nicco spun around to see her kicking her assailant in the gut with her heel, following up by cocking her hip and shooting out her leg. He looked stunned before he charged at her.

She dropped to her knees and hunched over. Moving too fast to halt his forward momentum, her assailant tripped over her. When he tried to get up, she locked up his elbow, then used it like a wrench to force him back to the floor.

Seizing her advantage, she pressed her forearm to his neck. He bucked beneath her, but she bore down until he lost consciousness, a move, Nicco knew, that rendered an opponent unconscious but didn't leave any permanent damage.

She looked up, flashed Nicco a grin.

Nicco brought out the plastic zip ties he routinely kept in his tactical vest and secured the hands of the first man, then the second. Nicco then turned the first one over and none-too-gently nudged him awake with the toe of his boot to the ribs. "One question."

The man blinked, then glared at Nicco and Scout with sullen eyes. "Yeah?"

"Why did you and your partner wait? Why not take me out earlier?" The question had bothered him from the moment he'd stepped inside Daniels's estate and reached Scout without encountering any tangos.

The second man came around and answered. "The boss lady. She said how we was supposed to let the bomb get you, but if it didn't, we was to kill you ourselves."

Nicco exchanged a glance with Scout.

"She's crazy, that one," the first man added. "She told us to take a video on our phones of you going *boom*. 'Course, you didn't. Go boom, I mean." He shook his head. "Boss lady's gonna be real mad about that." Suddenly, he brightened. "She'll be even madder when she learns we was recording the whole time she was giving us orders. She didn't know that. An insurance policy, so to speak, seeing as how she has a way of getting rid of the people who work for her."

Nicco fished inside the men's pockets and came

away with two cell phones. He tried one phone, found it password protected. "Password. Now."

The first man looked sullen. "Figure it out yourself."

Nicco widened his stance, stared down at the thug. "Password. I won't ask again."

The man spit out the password. "Happy?"

Nicco tapped it in, opened the phone, and saw the video the man had recorded. He repeated the process with the second man. "Now I'm happy."

He pulled out his own phone and dialed 911, explained the situation. "Suspects are secured." He thought of Daniels. "Send a coroner's van, too."

"These two aren't going anywhere," he said to Scout. "We'll leave them for the police." He flashed her a smile. "Newtown's in for some surprises."

"I always did love a surprise party."

Scout gripped the dashboard as Nicco took a fast left turn on the way to the hotel where the gala was being held. "I can't wait to see the Duchess's face when she realizes we're alive."

He didn't break every traffic rule, but he came close. "That's a party I don't want to miss." He slanted a grin at her. "Your stomach still in place?"

"I'll let you know when we get there."

"You're something else. First you get tied up, then a bomb is strapped to you, and you've still got your sass."

"Someone once told me I was Ranger-strong," she said.

"Someone was pretty smart."

Scout gave the video on the first man's phone a final glance and grinned. Newtown had had no idea that her thugs had been recording her. "If a picture is worth a thousand words, what's a video complete with sound worth?"

"I'd say twenty-five to life."

"I wonder how the Duchess feels about prison orange."

"We're about to find out." Nicco swung the truck into a parking space, and they both hopped out.

At the doorway to the ballroom, she showed the admission tickets to a man in hotel livery. He looked askance at her and Nicco's torn clothes but waved them through.

The party was in full swing when they arrived. Scout spotted Newtown on the raised dais along with the mayor, city council members, a congresswoman, and other dignitaries. The clink of crystal, the scent of expensive perfume, and the buzz of alcohol-infused chatter reminded her of the charity ball where she and Nicco had met.

She lifted her gaze to his, saw that he remembered as well.

Then, as now, the room was filled with beautiful people dressed in beautiful clothes and draped with jewel-studded gold and platinum. A string quartet provided discreetly muted background music, a suitable complement to the rich smell of hothouse flowers. To her mind, nothing could be more contrived, staged and altogether false. Not to mention mind-numbingly boring.

It occurred to Scout that the setting was much like Newtown herself—glossy, sophisticated, an illusion designed to deceive and to manipulate.

She and Nicco were about to change that.

As she took in the formal attire of the guests, she looked down at her own bedraggled clothes, hardly suitable for attending the city's biggest gala of the year, and grinned. "I think we're a trifle underdressed."

His mouth quirked at the understatement. "Yeah, we probably won't be making the best-dressed list."

"I'll try to bear up."

He took her arm and, together, they marched to the front of the room and climbed the short set of stairs to the dais. The party conversation gradually died, but curiosity at their appearance buzzed just below the surface.

Scout leaned across the table and got in Newtown's face. "Surprised to see us? You're done, Duchess. You'll be spending the rest of your life in a nine-by-nine cell. It'll be interesting to see how far your Lady Bountiful act takes you in a federal lockup."

Newtown's expression twisted before smoothing to glass as she turned to the mayor. "I don't know who these people are or what they want. Please have them removed."

The mayor made to stand when Nicco placed a hand on his shoulder, forcing him back to his seat. "You're going to want to take a look at this."

Bemusement turned to horror as the mayor watched the short video of Newtown giving orders to kill Nicco and Scout. "I don't know what to say." His gaze collided with Newtown's.

"It's fake," she said, chin raised to an arrogant angle. "A pitiful attempt by my enemies to discredit me and my work."

Scout leaned in closer. "We've got two witnesses to back it up. And if that isn't enough, Gerald Daniels's body with a bullet in his back. All courtesy of you, Duchess."

"How dare you? How dare you speak to me—Patrice Newtown—that way? You're nothing. Nothing, do you hear me?" She lifted her gaze to stare down those in attendance. "You are all nothing."

Those close enough to hear gasped in unison.

Newtown rose from her seat and raised her head imperiously. "Do you have any idea of how much good I've done for this city? There are charities that wouldn't even exist but for me. I won't serve a day. The people of Savannah will rise up in protest. They love me." She spread her arms wide, then closed them to embrace herself.

"We'll see how much they love you when they find out that you ordered the murders of two men," Nicco said. "And that's just for starters."

All semblance of the lady Newtown professed to be vanished as she unleashed the full extent of her fury on Scout. "You're a little nobody who thinks she can bring me down." She spread her arms wide. "Look at them. All of these people here to honor me. To worship me. They may call me *Duchess*, but I am their queen. Their queen, do you hear me?"

"You don't deserve honor. And you certainly don't deserve worship. There's only One who can claim that." Scout stared at the woman and saw the monster inside.

Newtown's pupils twitched, an involuntary reaction, part of the body's fight-or-flight instincts. The primal part of her recognized she was in danger, even if the cool and polished woman refused to admit it.

Her gaze darted from the mayor to the other

dignitaries on the dais. Whispers hummed through the air.

Newtown must have accepted that she was beaten for she made a break for it. Nicco started after her, but Scout stopped him. "She's mine."

Newtown darted behind the wall of curtains. Hot on her heels, Scout tackled her to the floor. After a brief scuffle, Scout grabbed Newtown by the elbow and yanked her to her feet.

"You're finished." She looked up to find Nicco grinning at her and giving her a thumbs-up.

By that time, the police, with Detective Wagner in the lead, had arrived. His gaze traveled from Scout to Nicco, who filled him in on what had happened and showed him the videos.

Wagner turned his attention to Newtown. "Patrice Newtown, you're under arrest for murder, conspiracy to commit murder, transportation of stolen weapons, and anything else I can think of. You have the right to remain silent. You have..."

Scout and Nicco left him to it to withdraw behind the curtains. "You took Newtown down like a pro," he said. "Remind me not to get on your bad side."

Scout brushed her fingers over the reddening scrape on his jaw from the fight with Newtown's henchman, stood on her tiptoes to press a kiss to it. "I think you're pretty safe there."

Now that Newtown was in custody and the

heart-pounding fear of the last hours was over, Scout felt more vulnerable than ever. Had Nicco really meant what he'd said just before cutting the last wires of the rigged vest? Or had the words been uttered in the heat of a tension-filled moment?

Adding to her uncertainty was the realization that he hadn't actually said the words *I love you*, only a casual "right back at you." She let her gaze move over him and saw the man she loved with all of her heart. Had it only been this morning that they'd hurled angry words at each other? So much had happened since then. Could she be sure of her feelings? And what of Nicco's?

"Did I thank you for saving my life…again?" she asked.

"Yeah. I'm pretty sure you did."

"I was wrong to leave the way I did."

"And I was wrong to order you to leave things to me," Nicco said. "That's not who you are. Not who I want you to be. I love you just as you are. Strong and courageous and independent. And so beautiful you take my breath away."

The last of her doubts vanished. She stood on her toes to press a kiss to his lips.

In turn, he skimmed his lips over her throat with its necklace of angry bruises from where one of the thugs had all but strangled her. "I love you."

It shot straight to her heart, the three simple words that sent her world spinning. They weakened her knees, turned her brain to mush. And her heart...her heart melted in a puddle of love. "I love you back."

He framed her face with his hands. "You are my everything."

"And you mine." Tears flooded her throat. Stung her eyes. And filled her heart. But they were healing tears. She touched a finger to her cheek. Found it wet.

Nicco brought her finger to his lips and licked away the tears. "I can't promise there won't be more tears. There will. They're part of life. But I can promise to love you every day for as long as I live." He released her finger to take her hand.

"Don't let go."

"Never."

Still holding her hand, he brought her to her toes, lowered his head to hers, and took her lips in a kiss so sweet, so tender that she wanted to weep from it. At the same time, she wanted to rejoice. Who knew it could be both? And more. So much more.

"Looks like we're pretty well matched," he said when he lifted his head.

"Perfectly." This time it was she who reached for him. "You have the right to tell me that you love me. Again."

"It would be my pleasure." And he did.

* * * * *

Dear Readers,

Thank you for joining me on another journey. I love writing about courageous men and women like Nicco and Scout. Their love path was a tortuous one as they battled enemies motivated by greed and power. In the end, love and truth won out.

Courage, like heroes, comes in all flavors. Some of the most courageous men and women I know are those who fight cancer. My mother and my sister fought ovarian cancer with humor and resolve and, most of all, faith. In spite of this, the cancer won, or at least it did on this earthly sphere. But I know it does not triumph beyond the grave. I remind myself of that when I am grieving and comfort myself with the knowledge that I am separated from them for only a brief time.

Nicco and Scout also lost loved ones. Like me, they grieved, sometimes unbearably so, and they searched for ways to continue living. When their strength faltered, they relied upon the Lord and found in Him the strength and the will to go on.

I pray that you can turn to the Lord in whatever battles you face.

With gratitude for His love,
Jane

Get 2 Free Books,
Plus 2 Free Gifts—
just for trying the Reader Service!

Love Inspired®

Get 2 Free Books,
Plus 2 Free Gifts—
just for trying the Reader Service!

HARLEQUIN®

HEARTWARMING™

HW17R2

HOME *on the* RANCH

YES! Please send me the **Home on the Ranch Collection** in Larger Print. This collection begins with 3 FREE books and 2 FREE gifts in the first shipment. Along with my 3 free books, I'll also get the next 4 books from the Home on the Ranch Collection, in LARGER PRINT, which I may either return and owe nothing, or keep for the low price of $5.24 U.S./ $5.89 CDN each plus $2.99 for shipping and handling per shipment*. If I decide to continue, about once a month for 8 months I will get 6 or 7 more books, but will only need to pay for 4. That means 2 or 3 books in every shipment will be FREE! If I decide to keep the entire collection, I'll have paid for only 32 books because 19 books are FREE! I understand that accepting the 3 free books and gifts places me under no obligation to buy anything. I can always return a shipment and cancel at any time. My free books and gifts are mine to keep no matter what I decide.

268 HCN 3760 468 HCN 3760

Name	(PLEASE PRINT)	
Address		Apt. #
City	State/Prov.	Zip/Postal Code

Signature (if under 18, a parent or guardian must sign)

Mail to the **Reader Service**:
IN U.S.A.: P.O. Box 1867, Buffalo, NY. 14240-1867
IN CANADA: P.O. Box 609, Fort Erie, Ontario L2A 5X3

* Terms and prices subject to change without notice. Prices do not include applicable taxes. Sales tax applicable in NY. Canadian residents will be charged applicable taxes. This offer is limited to one order per household. All orders subject to approval. Credit or debit balances in a customer's account(s) may be offset by any other outstanding balance owed by or to the customer. Please allow 3 to 4 weeks for delivery. Offer available while quantities last. Offer not available to Quebec residents.

Your Privacy—The Reader Service is committed to protecting your privacy. Our Privacy Policy is available online at www.ReaderService.com or upon request from the Reader Service.

We make a portion of our mailing list available to reputable third parties that offer products we believe may interest you. If you prefer that we not exchange your name with third parties, or if you wish to clarify or modify your communication preferences, please visit us at www.ReaderService.com/consumerschoice or write to us at Reader Service Preference Service, P.O. Box 9062, Buffalo, NY. 14240-9062. Include your complete name and address.

HRCBPA18

Get 2 Free Books,
<u>Plus</u> 2 Free Gifts –

just for trying the *Reader Service!*